bats and bones:

A Frannie Shoemaker Campground Mystery

by Karen Musser Nortman

Cover Artwork by Gretchen Musser
Cover Design by Libby Shannon

This is a work of fiction. Names, characters, places and incidents are either the product of the author's imagination, or are used fictitiously, and any resemblance to actual persons, living or dead, business establishments, events, or locales is purely coincidental. Except for Cuba, who has now gone to the Land of Three-Legged Rabbits.

Dedication

To Butch, my favorite camping buddy

The Frannie Shoemaker Campground Mysteries

Bats and Bones
The Blue Coyote
Peete and Repeat
The Lady of the Lake
To Cache a Killer
A Campy Christmas
The Space Invader
We Are NOT Buying a Camper! (prequel)

The Time Travel Trailer Series

The Time Travel Trailer
Trailer on the Fly

TABLE OF CONTENTS

Chapter One	1
Chapter Two	10
Chapter Three	20
Chapter Four	29
Chapter Five	41
Chapter Six	54
Chapter Seven	68
Chapter Eight	78
Chapter Nine	91
Chapter Ten	106
Chapter Eleven	122
Chapter Twelve	139
Chapter Thirteen	153
Chapter Fourteen	172
Chapter Fifteen	192
Chapter Sixteen	209
Happy Camper Tips	229
Other Books by the Author	235
Thanks...	239
Acknowledgments	240
About the Author	241

Chapter One

Friday Afternoon

A LARGE NEW MOTORHOME pulled forward into a campsite. Two forty-something men climbed out of the front, one laughing and the other definitely not. At the same time the side door opened and four more men spilled out, all appearing to be in the same age range. Several beer cans rolled out the door as the last man emerged, laughed raucously, slapped the man ahead of him on the back, and stooped to pick up the cans and heave them back in the coach. Whereupon they rolled right back out and the man laughed even harder.

Frannie Shoemaker, her husband Larry, and their fellow campers relaxed in lawn chairs at their campsite across the road, trying to stay cool in the July heat and humidity. Shoemakers' old yellow Lab, Cuba, sprawled at their side. They halted their conversation as the spectacle became more riveting.

Mickey Ferraro, Frannie's brother-in-law, sat forward in his chair. "Oh, brother, it could be a long night for them—and for us—unless they pass out. At least the driver looks sober." One of the men pulled out the electrical cord, but the post was at the opposite corner and the cord didn't reach. Two of them conferred and searched the storage compartments while the others hauled out lawn chairs and coolers.

The driver, a large ruddy man with thinning blond hair, straightened up and pointed at the Shoemakers and their friends. He ambled across the road and stuck out a hand to Larry. "Stub Berger," he said. He looked as if he may have been athletic in his youth but had gone to fat in middle age.

Larry shook his hand. "Larry. What's your problem?"

"Well, Lar, I wonder if any of you might have an extension cord we could borrow. We'll only be here overnight."

"I'm sure we do. But why did you pull in that direction?" Larry asked.

Stub looked puzzled so Mickey added, "Most people back in unless they want their door to face another unit. If you back in, your cord will be plenty long. Did you just get that coach?"

"Rented it. Over south of Chicago. Me and my buddies are on a two week stag trip—headed out west."

Mickey asked, "Have any of you ever camped before?"

Stub laughed. "Naw, we're all newbies. Well, I went to scout camp as a kid."

One of Stub's companions holding a loop of hose hailed him just then. "Hey, Stub! Ask them where the water hook-up is."

Stub looked back at Shoemakers' group. Larry said, "These sites are electrical only. This is an old campground. You have to fill up with water back there." He pointed up the hill at the spigot.

"Oh, man," Stub slapped himself on the forehead. "Well, I guess if I go back to get water, I can back it in and won't need a cord. Thanks for the info." He hurried back to the big RV.

The Shoemakers' group all looked at each other, did a little eyebrow raising and resisted laughing out loud. They continued watching the scene unfold across the road. After his buddies moved all of the chairs and coolers out of the way, Stub backed the motorhome out and drove back up the road to find a spot to turn around.

Soon the motorhome faced them at the top of the hill and a couple of the other men hauled the hose up to fill the tank. Laughter and curses drifted down on the occasional teasing puff of wind, and after much ado, Stub proceeded back down the hill. It took four attempts to back the coach in before the group either gave up or was satisfied and pronounced the deed done.

For the long Fourth of July weekend, Frannie and Larry had anticipated relaxing and exploring the trails among the bluffs of Bat Cave State Park. The natural beauty and peace of Bat Cave more than compensated for the small campground and the old shower house. Stands of white pine and hardwood backed each site and smaller understory trees and shrubs bordered the sides, giving the sites more privacy than most campgrounds. This part of eastern Iowa had escaped the glaciers of the last ice age and the resulting limestone bluffs and caves presented vistas totally unlike the cornfields viewed from I-80.

Frannie stretched and felt her anxieties lift. The weekend extended ahead with basically no responsibilities. Cleaning? She didn't keep a vacuum in the camper—too bad. Cooking? Very little and that was part of the entertainment. Beautiful surroundings, good conversation with friends, a little walking or hiking, a good book, and an occasional glass of wine made the best antidote she knew to the grief that still nagged her over the recent loss of her mother.

"When are Nowaks supposed to get here?" Mickey asked.

Larry looked at his watch. "About a half-hour, I think." Larry surveyed their site, hands on hips, in what Frannie called his 'police pose.' He had retired five years earlier from a small town police force. Both he and his sister, Jane Ann Ferraro, were tall and slender—the blessings of genetics plus an active lifestyle—and Larry maintained ramrod posture and gray hair in a military buzz cut that still managed to convey an air of benign authority.

They settled back in their lawn chairs while the unpacking and head scratching continued with Stub's group. Before long, Rob and Donna Nowak arrived pulling a new trailer. They soon had it backed into the site next to Stub, and Larry and Mickey wandered over to help with the setup.

"Hey, campers! Are you ready for the weekend?" Rob, a small wiry man sporting a goatee, greeted the men

4

as they approached. "Wow! This is a beautiful place! The campsites are so secluded. So glad you guys invited us."

"We like it," said Larry. "Wait until you see the cave area."

Frannie and Jane Ann had remained in their chairs and Frannie mumbled, "Invited? Donna overheard us discussing plans a few weeks ago and asked if she and Rob could come."

"She's not shy," Jane Ann said. "Although I have to admit, I don't know her all that well."

"Well, me neither, but I guess as well as I ever wanted to. She's pretty high-maintenance," Frannie said. "But... I'd better make the effort." She got up, followed by Jane Ann, to greet the newcomers.

Donna Nowak stood, arms akimbo and, with her round shape and spiky blonde hair, brought to mind a hand grenade. She gave sharp directions to Rob, which he cheerfully ignored. Finally, she followed Frannie and Jane Ann back across the road at their invitation, trailing her feisty schnauzer, Buster, behind her on his leash.

The Shoemaker fire ring and picnic table had been chosen as the gathering spot. The group had planned a cold potluck supper for later with dishes they had prepared at home. At this point, the oppressive heat dulled any appetites. Cuba and even Buster stretched in the shade, tongues hanging in the dirt.

Donna leaned over to Frannie. "I was really sorry to hear about your mom. She had been sick awhile, hadn't she?"

Frannie swallowed a lump. "Yes, she had been living with us several months until we had to move her to the nursing home. She only lived a week...."

Donna interrupted. "So you had been taking care of her quite awhile? Probably all for the best, then."

Frannie hated that phrase. Define best. But she hastened to change the subject. "Do you and Rob camp fairly often?"

"Oh, yes. We've been to a lot of the state parks in Iowa but we like to go to private campgrounds. They generally have nicer facilities and full hookups."

"They're usually more expensive...," Frannie said but had no chance to finish.

"Yeah, but not that bad. We've thought about getting a seasonal site and just staying the same place all summer — you know, get to know people and not have to haul the camper out and back home every weekend. But we like to visit the local wineries and other sites in different places."

The men returned after completing the setup and conversation ebbed and flowed as they all watched new arrivals and bemoaned the heat. Finally, Jane Ann announced that she thought it was time to eat.

The group busied themselves setting the table and carrying bowls and plates out of their little refrigerators and coolers. Soon they sat down to a spread of fresh rolls, assorted salads, marinated cold roast beef, fresh fruit and everyone's own choice of wine served in the finest plastic stemware. The table sported bright paper plates on a red checked tablecloth. Jane Ann had brought a small bouquet of daisies, black-eyed Susans, and Russian sage from home and stuck them in a Ball jar.

"Jane Ann, could you get me a serving spoon for this salad?" Donna asked. "I forgot to bring one over from our camper."

Jane Ann nodded, caught Frannie's eye, and went back in to find the requested implement.

The breeze had picked up a little and the angled rays of the sun filtered through the tall pines, transforming the understory into a shimmering gold.

Mickey raised his glass. "A toast!" he said, "to those poor souls forced to eat inside tonight at some overpriced restaurant. They don't know what they're missing."

"Hear, hear!" the others chorused and clicked their glasses.

Donna said, "Actually, we usually go out somewhere to eat when we're camping. It's a lot easier."

"But we're better cooks than most restaurants," Mickey said, grinning.

"Oh, I don't know," Donna said. "We've been to some pretty good places, haven't we, honey?" She looked at Rob.

Rob fidgeted. "Yeah...some good ones, but this is excellent. And Mickey's right—the ambience can't be beat."

Donna said, "Restaurants do have air-conditioning." Frannie wondered again why Donna had wanted to be here.

Larry looked offended. "We have air-conditioning," he said. "And no doubt we will all fire it up when we go to bed."

"Is it time to go to bed yet?" Donna asked, mopping her brow with her napkin. She really did look a little overheated.

Frannie scooped another helping of the corn and snagged a roll as the basket passed. "Not while we still have that corn salad and those rolls. Donna, you will be required to bring those rolls on every trip." She paused as she realized what she said, then hurried on. "And I happen to know that Mickey has one of his famous apple cobblers stashed in his camper."

"We have ice cream, too—stopped at that great little place on the way up that's been there for years and makes their own. . ." Jane Ann's voice trailed off at the sound of raised voices coming from across the road. A black pickup pulling a fifth-wheel trailer sat in the road. The driver stood at the post that held the reservation card and the site number for Stub's campsite. A short, gray-haired woman talked loudly and pointed at Stub and a couple of his fellow travelers. The driver looked rather embarrassed, but Stub raised his hands in surrender. The driver climbed up in his truck and the woman marched away toward the center of the campground.

"What's that about?" Larry wondered.

Mickey smirked. "Well, Lar, I think your old buddy Stub may be in the wrong site."

"You're right," Frannie said. "That woman is the campground host. I saw her earlier when I walked the dog."

Sure enough, the pickup with the fifth wheel pulled forward to reveal Stub and his friends hastily gathering up lawn chairs and other paraphernalia. The grumpy man slammed chairs closed and threw cans back in coolers.

Stub got back in the driver's seat of the motorhome and started to pull out. Larry jumped up from the picnic table and waved his arms. "Wait!" he yelled.

He loped across the road toward the coach. "What the hell...?" Mickey said.

Jane Ann pointed at the electrical post. "He didn't unplug it!"

Chapter Two

THE CORD PULLED TAUT and then jerked out of the post just as Larry got there. Stub stopped the motorhome and rolled down the window, his usually jovial expression replaced with confusion and concern.

Larry pointed at the cord. "You forgot to unplug your electrical hook up."

Stub banged his head down on the steering wheel, fortunately cushioned by his hands. Raising his head again, he looked at Larry. "Oh, man, what did I do? Did I wreck something?"

"I'll check. Don't move any farther." With that Larry headed to the back of the coach and picked up the end of the cord. He examined the plug and shook his head back at Stub. "It looks okay — the prongs are a little bent but it should work fine. I'll stow it for you." He began to push the cord back into its compartment. Stub's fellow travelers had stopped their frantic packing up. Grumpy, a small, thin man with a prematurely receding hairline and wire rim glasses, said, "This trip is Stub's worst idea ever!"

"Relax, Randy," another man said. "Nothing's hurt. We'll get moved to the right spot and start over. It's not that bad."

Randy's face reddened, and he started to retort but apparently thought better of it. He threw down a lawn chair, said, "I'm going to the can!" and marched off toward the shower house. Larry had finished with the cord and walked back to the driver's window. "You're good to go now. Been there, done that. Are you in the wrong spot?"

Stub sighed. "Yeah, we didn't check the reservation number on the site and we're supposed to be on the other side of your friends." He nodded at the Nowaks' unit.

Larry nodded toward Randy trudging down the road. "Your friend seems really upset."

"Don't mind Randy. He's a little uptight right now— the Feds are after him." Then noticing Larry's jaw drop, Stub added, "Tax problems."

"Bummer. Well, I'll let you get back to your move. Think of it as practice."

Stub chuckled. "Hey, thanks…for everything!"

Larry nodded and headed back across the road. He managed to keep a straight face all the way to the picnic table. "Good thing supper started out cold," he said to the group.

"What's the scoop?" Rob asked. "Do they have to leave or just move?"

"They're just in the wrong spot. They are supposed to be on the other side of you." Larry then repeated what Stub had said about Randy. "I thought at first he was on the run from the FBI, but apparently he's in trouble with the IRS."

"Those guys oughta be in a movie," Donna said. "I can't imagine they'll make it two weeks without killing each other."

Frannie got up from the table. "Ladies, I propose a stroll around the campground and let the men clean up."

"I'm up for it," Jane Ann said, "although we're letting them off easy with paper plates."

The women leashed up the dogs and ambled along the road. The temperature discouraged brisk walking. Just past the shower house, they spotted the hosts' camper. The usual official park host sign marked the site, but keeping it company were a four-foot plastic lamppost with a swinging sign announcing "The Schlumms — Dave and Maeve," a stars and stripes windsock, three spinning yard ornaments, four sets of wind chimes, a bird feeder, a large bright green artificial turf rug and a wooden cutout Uncle Sam who appeared to be lecturing to a pink plastic flamingo. The woman who had confronted Stub and his friends was now arguing with a short sturdy older man with a shock of thick white hair.

"I'm just saying, you could be a little more tactful," he offered.

"Who cares? I'm sick of this whole gig. These people are too lazy to even read the signs!" She had not cooled off much but struggled to keep her voice down.

"Well, it won't be for much longer — you've seen to that." He went in the camper and slammed the door.

Frannie and the other women kept moving until they were out of earshot. Frannie raised her eyebrows. "Dave and Maeve? Really?"

Donna said, "Maybe they just made it up for this host 'gig'."

"Apparently the 'gig' is almost up, so to speak," Jane Ann said.

Frannie groaned. "Doesn't sound like a scheduled end either. I wonder what's up."

Across the road, Donna pointed at a couple of odd-shaped tents. "Check those out!" The small tents were half perched on small-wheeled trailers and half on the ground, forming a step shape.

"I bet those belong to bikers," Jane Ann said. "The tent folds out of the little pull-behind trailer. You have a bed in the trailer section and a stand up area on the ground where you can change clothes and store stuff."

"Wow!" Donna said. "That's cool! Not that I'm about to give up my new trailer, but they look neat."

The women reached the end of the campground and headed back. Many campsites sported American flags and patriotic ornaments in observance of the holiday weekend. Jane Ann's cell phone rang and she stopped, pulled the phone out of her pocket and moved slightly away from the other two. Frannie had caught the look of concern as her sister-in-law answered the call and distracted Donna by pointing out some children in one site preparing to light sparklers.

A moment later, Jane Ann turned back to them, frown lines gone and the usual glow returned to her face.

"That was Mona," she said to Frannie. "She said it was uncomfortable at first but things are going well, and she misses us."

Jane Ann and Mickey had adopted young sisters as toddlers. Now in their twenties, the girls had grown into delightful, responsible young women and out of the blue had recently embarked on an effort to meet their birth mother. Mickey and Jane Ann had given them somewhat reluctant support and helped them arrange a reunion this weekend. It was part of the reason Larry and Frannie had suggested the camping trip. Jane Ann had confided to Frannie that while she naturally felt a little threatened, she was more concerned that the girls were building up expectations that may be crushed.

"Of course she misses you," Frannie assured her. "And Justine is getting along okay too?"

Jane Ann nodded and explained the situation to Donna. Once enlightened, she was uncharacteristically quiet the rest of the walk.

As they neared their campsites, they spotted Rob perched precariously on a small stepladder with strings of lights in both hands and around his neck.

"I almost forgot about Rob's new lights," Donna said. "Wait till you see this—he's gone totally wacko this time." Rob obsessed over his outdoor lighting. Their remodeled ranch house sported special decorative lights for every season, holiday, and Rob's favorite sports teams, and he outdid himself with their travel trailer. While Rob worked, Mickey and Larry sprawled in their lawn chairs each enjoying a beer and Frannie got out a tin of dominos.

"Chicken Feet, anyone?" she asked. Jane Ann joined her at the picnic table for the simple game. Donna said she didn't like games and opted to keep an eye on her husband's exertions across the road.

"He reminds me of that squirrel that annoyed us so much last fall," Larry said. Rob had strung small American flag lights along the awning and outlined the bottom of the trailer and the steps with strings of red, white and blue lights. Then he assembled a portable lamppost at the corner of their campsite and ran a wire back under the outdoor rug to the external outlet on the trailer. Finally, he plugged everything in and the twilight blazed with a garish display of red, white and blue. The lamppost glowed white, faded, blazed red, faded again, burned royal blue and repeated the cycle. His camping mates clapped and gave a couple of shrill whistles.

"I'm not done yet!" Rob disappeared into the camper. He reappeared with a small speaker and placed it on their utility table. Then he bounded back inside. Suddenly the humid evening air filled with the stirring sounds of "Stars and Stripes Forever" as the lights flashed and cavorted to the beat of the march.

As Rob reappeared flush and beaming, mopping the sweat off his forehead, Mickey burst out in deep laughter, Larry whistled and clapped again, and the women, after a moment of speechlessness, joined in. Meanwhile, Stub's group, now relocated, came into the road laughing and pointing. Stub came over and slapped Rob on the backwhile shoving a beer at him. Rob accepted it gratefully while the rest of Stub's group showered him with praise for his artistic achievement. Frannie stood shaking her head, speechless.

Donna shrugged. "I can't control him."

A small boy slowly rounded the end of Frannie and Larry's trailer. He looked to be about five, had brown spiky hair and wore baggy denim shorts and an oversized T-shirt, both grubby. He stared with open mouth at the display. He slowly pivoted to address the women hooting behind him.

"That is awesome!"

Frannie grinned at Donna. "No accounting for taste."

"Do you know him?" the boy said.

"I'm afraid so," Donna said. "He's my husband. Are you camping next door?"

"Yeah. I think my dad's going to do lights like that!" He spotted Buster straining on his leash. "Is that your dog?"

"Guilty on two counts. His name is Buster. Would you like to pet him? He's very friendly."

The boy fell to his knees and wrapped his arms around Buster's neck. Buster promptly paid for the affection with several licks of the boy's face. The boy began to giggle and struggled to his feet.

"What's your name?" Frannie asked.

"River. My dad's going to get me a dog like that!"

"River? Like a stream?"

He shrugged his shoulders. "A what? It's just my name!"

"River!" A voice came from the other side of the Shoemakers' trailer.

"Gotta go! See ya, Buster!" and he took off.

As they watched him go, they also saw the hostess, Maeve, marching down the road headed toward Rob and Donna's trailer.

"Uh-oh," Donna said and went to join her husband. She reached Rob's side just as Maeve planted her short stocky body, hands on hips, in front of him. Her frizzy grey hair shook as she issued orders.

"Turn that off! We have quiet hours in this park!"

Rob looked sheepish. "I thought not until 10:00, right? It's only 8:30, but I will turn it down. I was just trying it out—sorry."

"You can't cause a disturbance like that anytime!" Maeve insisted, getting almost in Rob's face.

"Give the guy a break! You and your stupid rules!" Randy had moved up behind Maeve, accompanied by Stub.

Stub was more conciliatory. "He said he would turn it down, ma'am. He's not bothering us."

Maeve spun around to face Stub. "You are not the only campers here, despite what you may think!" She gyrated on her heel and marched back up the road.

"She's pretty crabby," Stub said.

"Crabby? She's a bitch!" Randy said, and stomped off in the other direction.

Stub shrugged, hands palm up. "The ranger told us that they have been asked to leave at the end of next week because so many people have complained about her."

"Ohhh—" Donna said, "we overheard a bit of conversation between her and her husband when we were on our walk. That explains it."

"Well," Rob said, "I for one am ready to kick back in my chair for the rest of the evening. Camping is supposed to be relaxing right?" He added to Donna. "Ready, Punkin?"

Donna grinned and winked at him. "Better turn your music off first."

Soon the group was back at the empty fire ring and spent a relatively quiet hour rehashing the events since their arrival. Around 9:30, they heard a loud rumble down the road toward the entrance. The roar grew and two huge shiny Harleys came into view. Each had two riders, a man and a woman, dressed in leathers and do-rags, gray hair in ponytails or flying wildly behind them. All four waved at the campers, who responded in kind.

"Must be the owners of the funny tents," Donna said.

"But they still have to run the gauntlet," Mickey said. He nodded down toward the host site. Sure enough, Maeve stood by the road, hands on hips, with a glare louder than the bikes. As they passed, she followed them to their campsite, disappearing around the corner of the road.

"Glad we're not within earshot of that," Frannie said. "I think there's been enough excitement tonight for the whole weekend."

Jane Ann stood up and gathered her book and wine glass, folded her chair and announced, "I'm ready for bed and some decadent air conditioning. See you all in the morning."

The others gradually followed suit after making tentative plans to hike the cave paths in the morning.

"The ranger said the caves are closed right now because they're afraid of that white-nosed bat syndrome being spread to bats here but the trails are open," Larry said.

Frannie shuddered. "I certainly don't need to go in the caves for a fulfilling nature experience. C'mon, Cuba — time for bed." The old Lab slowly got to her feet, stretched and trotted toward the trailer. Larry soon followed.

As Larry and Frannie prepared for bed, Larry looked at her seriously.

"How are you getting along with Donna? I heard her ask about your mom."

"It's okay. She probably means well—it just doesn't come off that way. But tonight was so crazy, Donna couldn't really compete with everything else going on."

"That's for sure! Let's hope the rest of the weekend is a little quieter." He kissed her and headed to brush his teeth. Frannie decided she was too tired to read, switched off her light, and dozed off to the hum of the AC.

Chapter Three

Early Saturday Morning

THE NEXT MORNING, FRANNIE picked her way down the steps of the trailer balancing the percolator to avoid bouncing and waking her husband. The campground appeared quiet, although the campsites were so secluded in the pines, ash and maples, it was hard to tell. The air was heavy and sticky following the record heat and humidity of the previous day. She plugged the coffee pot into the outside outlet and placed it on the metal utility table.

Grabbing the leash out of a sealed tub, she took Cuba around the campground to take care of necessary chores. Finally, settled in a camp chair with her book, she listened to the sounds of the morning. The sun was just beginning to filter gold through some of the understory trees and shrubs. Occasionally a mischievous breeze tickled a few leaves, ignoring others. The percolator gurgled and wheezed in spasms until it crescendoed into that final effort to present her first caffeine of the day.

This was her favorite time of the day, anywhere really, but especially in a campground. Usually a few people were stirring, but for the most part little disturbed the morning quiet.

A truck door slammed and she looked up to see a red pickup back out of the space across the road and several sites down. The truck then peeled out at a speed not quite up to the standards of a newly licensed teenager but certainly more than dramatic enough for a campground.

The night before, they had noticed the pickup next to a new Airstream, fresh and shiny and comfortable in its retro good looks.

"That is so cool--we should go over and ask if we can see inside," Larry had said as he sipped a beer and stood frankly staring. A group of six or seven people of varying ages had been laughing, eating and enjoying a campfire near the Airstream.

"Can you do that?" Rob had asked.

"Sure," Jane Ann said. "Most people consider it a compliment. Those people next to us two weeks ago wanted to see ours."

"Ha!" Mickey said. "With our luck the guy would be a serial killer or something."

Now Frannie smiled at the thought. Most of the campgrounds she and Larry frequented were not exactly hotbeds of wild characters, let alone felons. Although there had been a few odd ducks...She read for a while, occasionally looking up at the sound of a bird in a nearby tree or rustling in the woods.

Eventually the screen door of Nowaks' trailer opened and Donna emerged carrying Buster. Speaking of odd ducks...

"Good morning!" Donna called, placing Buster on the ground and deftly grabbing his leash before he could escape. He strained at the leash and Cuba slowly raised her head and lowered it again with a sigh, not interested in the antics of youngsters.

"Be right back!" Donna said.

"Coffee's on," Frannie said, grimacing inwardly at having her quiet time disturbed.

Donna waved acknowledgement as Buster pulled her out on the campground road. The morning parade began soon after, as people from campsites further down headed for the shower house. Although most RV units have bathrooms, the limited size of tanks and water heaters encourages the use of campground facilities. The pilgrims were arrayed in attire as outlandish as any seen anywhere. A woman in Sponge Bob pajama bottoms, a 'wear pink' t-shirt, and turban from an olive green towel tottered along on spike heels, no less. Maybe she came here directly from work and forgot to put other shoes in, thought Frannie. A small boy clomped along in cowboy boots and a t-shirt down to his knees. A man at his side, presumably the boy's father, sported khaki shorts and a flopping Iowa Hawkeye robe, a towel that looked like some variation of Disney princesses around his neck. Two young girls, possibly sisters, shuffled along in the ubiquitous flip-flops, the bigger one madly texting a message of great import on her phone, her face hidden by long stringy hair, the smaller one poking her sister in the back with her toothbrush. All carried their grooming necessities in plastic grocery sacks, florescent-colored buckets, drawstring bags, or just gripped in one hand.

The screen door of the Shoemaker trailer opened and Larry bounced down the steps, coffee mug in hand.

He eyed the percolator. "Did I hear the magic words?"

"Just finished," Frannie said. Larry ambled over to the table and poured a cup, adding a couple of packets of sweetener. He then dragged another camp chair over next to Frannie.

"Certainly don't need a fire this morning to ward off the chill," he said. Instead of his usual early morning outfit of sweatpants and hooded sweatshirt, he wore baggy shorts and a T-shirt that looked like the raccoons had been at it. "How about breakfast? Are we cooking?"

Frannie shook her head. "I think it's a cereal and muffin morning. Too hot to cook already," she said. "Besides, we want to hike the Cave Trail before it gets even hotter."

"Good idea," he agreed.

Sometimes they planned elaborate breakfasts—eggs, sausage, pancakes, all cooked over the fire, or a favorite: "smashed potatoes," with sausage gravy, accompanied by juice or fresh fruit. But in warm or rainy weather, or when they had plans before noon, simpler fare sufficed. As the others emerged from their campers, Frannie went in hers to gather the breakfast makings for Larry and herself.

They had purchased their travel trailer five years earlier from a used camper lot. Frannie had amused herself and their friends with a complete but low cost makeover with a cozy rustic theme. She had recovered the fold down couch and dining benches with denim, hung homespun curtains, and added a couple of small wrought iron lamps. A stenciled border with moose and

23

bears, a hand-quilted lap robe in navy, red, and green prints and a couple of pillows made from old jeans complete with pockets finished the look. She loved the warm feeling, and even more the efficiency and simple upkeep, of the result.

She loaded a wooden tray with old plastic plates and bowls, flatware, cereal, bananas, butter and a basket of rhubarb almond muffins that she had snagged from her home freezer. As she struggled with the screen door, Larry jumped up from his spot at the picnic table to help her. Jane Ann had already brought out fresh strawberries, yogurt, and granola, while Rob contributed more cereal and toast, along with homemade apple butter.

Donna had returned from walking Buster and they all found seats around the table.

"I don't see much action from Stub's group this morning." Donna said.

"I got up about 1:30 and I could still see several out there around their fire," Mickey said.

Frannie looked over at Stub's campsite. "I thought they were taking off this morning."

"They still have four hours left of the morning," Jane Ann said.

"Speaking of that, who's up for hiking the trail before it gets too hot?" Rob asked.

There were no abstainers and they cleared their breakfast materials, piling the few dishes in their respective sinks. Shortly after, equipped with water bottles, sunglasses, cameras, and cell phones, they headed down the hill toward the trailhead, Buster in the lead and Cuba in tow.

"Have you guys ever been to that Rock Cliff Winery that's near here?" Donna asked as they walked down the middle of the road.

Jane Ann looked at Mickey. "I don't think so. Do you remember?"

"We've never been to one around here."

"We were thinking about going this afternoon," Donna said.

"Good idea," Frannie said. "We printed out a listing of the area events this weekend before we came. I think one of the small towns nearby is having a melon festival this weekend. And there's a band concert in town tomorrow night at the city park with fireworks after."

Jane Ann added, "There's also a log cabin here in the park—the first white settlers in the county. We haven't been to that for a couple of years but it was always well maintained. It's a hike through the woods so it's not touristy."

"Sounds like plenty to do," Donna said. "And even better if it cools off tomorrow. I've had it with this heat."

About a quarter mile from the campground, the road widened to a parking area with a small information kiosk. Wooden steps and walkways led off both sides of the lot down to a ravine lined with limestone walls. A small but lively stream wandered through the bottom of the ravine, disappearing in places into small caves and cascading over rocks in others. Trees and shrubs of all sizes, improbably growing out of the rocks, combined with the steep walls to create a welcoming shady retreat from the overheated promise of the day.

As the group proceeded single file down the steps to begin the trail on the north branch, they noticed a definite drop in the temperature.

Donna stared around her. "Wow, it's lovely here! Hard to believe we're in Iowa."

"Isn't it amazing?" Jane Ann said. "The biggest cave is over there on the left—the Colossus. The entrance is down those steps."

"I know we can't go in but we can go down to it, can't we?" Donna asked.

"Why not? The ranger didn't mention any restrictions on the trails," Rob said. They followed the steps down to the entrance of Colossus, stopping to snap photos of the contorted rocks and varied plants along the way.

Frannie examined each of plants around the entrance to the cave looking for wildflowers that she could identify. She stepped gingerly over the rocks off the path to avoid any debilitating accidents. She had learned the hard way that the older she got, the less reliable her balance. Jane Ann photographed Rob and Donna sitting on a boulder by the yawning entrance.

"I'm surprised they don't have any ropes or tape across the entrance," Rob said. "The ranger said they don't think the bats here have this white-nose syndrome yet but they are afraid people will carry it here."

"I guess they are counting on an honor system and don't want to junk up the place," Larry said.

Dragging Buster and Cuba from tantalizing olfactory possibilities in nooks and crannies, they continued along the path, peeking in small, shallow caves with names like The Closet, Cubbyhole, and Suitcase, and bigger caves named the Maze, the Saloon and Budge. The warmth of the sun at the bottom of this ravine was welcome, not oppressive like in the upper world. The little stream tumbled merrily along magnifying the varied stones at its bottom. The bobbing and twirling leaves of the shrubs and trees provided the capping idyllic element.

While the rest explored the area around one of the small caves, Frannie sat down on a rock by the stream, stripped off her shoes and socks and dangled her feet in the water. The stream was spring-fed and the icy cold took a few minutes of cringing adjustment. Then she leaned back and watched the bugs and dust motes dancing in the sunlight. The peace of the moment made the ruckus of the night before seem like a corny B movie. She dried her feet on an old bandana in her pocket and put her shoes and socks back on. As she got up and dusted off the back of her shorts, the rest started to move on and she stepped in behind the parade.

One of the last caves was farther up the side of the ravine and approached by a combination of graduated stones and short wooden walkways. It appeared to be one of the medium sized caves with a couple of large boulders covering about a third of the entrance.

"What's the name of this one?" Donna asked.

"The sign was back there before we started the climb. Bogg's Retreat," Mickey said.

As they peered inside trying to spot interesting formations in the gloom, Buster strained at the leash. Rob pulled him back, but he began barking at the mouth of the cave. The noise piqued Cuba's interest and she too pulled toward the cave. Buster managed to reach the boulders and rutted at a small pile of rocks, causing several to tumble and roll down the sloping entrance.

Donna gasped, echoed by several others. Protruding from the pile of rocks appeared to be a human toe.

Chapter Four

Mid-Saturday Morning

THEY ALL BEGAN TO talk at once and the dogs promptly went crazy. Larry handed Cuba's leash to Mickey and took charge.

"Everyone stay here. Don't move!" he said, and approached the cave around the open side of the boulders. Always prepared, Frannie thought, as he pulled a small flashlight from one of his cargo pockets and held it overhead, aiming it down behind the boulders.

"I think it's the host lady," he said. "And I don't think there's much chance but, Jane Ann, will you come up and see if she has a pulse?"

Donna nudged Rob. "You should go see," she said in a loud whisper. Rob hesitated, looking uncomfortable. Larry heard her.

"Not now, Donna. I just want Jane Ann to check for signs of life, and then we'll have to wait for the authorities," he said. Donna folded her arms and looked away, offended. But soon she craned her neck back toward the cave.

Jane Ann followed Larry's route and stepped around him, stopping for just an instant as fresh shock played over her face when she saw what he revealed with his light. Then she became all business and ducked behind the boulders. They could hear her calling Maeve Schlumm's name, trying to get a response.

Larry said, "Be careful not to touch anything you don't have to."

Jane Ann stood, her face washed of color, and shook her head. "She's gone."

Larry and Jane Ann exited the cave and Larry pulled out his cell phone to call 911. He shook his head and looked at his phone. "No signal here. I probably need to go back up to the parking lot."

"Can I come with you?" Frannie asked. Larry hesitated and then, seeing her forlorn face, nodded.

"Everyone else stay here, though, and don't let anyone near this place. We'll turn anyone back that we meet, but there may be hikers coming from the other way."

Donna interrupted. "Is it really the host lady?"

Larry and Jane Ann both nodded. "She's wearing the same clothes she had on last night," Jane Ann said.

Frannie felt numb. The little she knew of Maeve Schlumm from the night before couldn't be farther from the warm personality of her own mother, but somehow Maeve's death made the recent loss of her mother fresh and raw. The pleasant warmth of the morning and the ravine seemed to dissipate under a gray chill. She fell in behind Larry as he headed down the path.

"How did she die, could you tell?" Frannie asked.

"Her head had been bashed in on one side."

"Do you think she fell?"

Larry shrugged. "Possible."

"But why would she have been out here last night? We saw her go after those bikers and it was almost 10:00, so it must have been after that."

"Maybe it was this morning—she might have put the same clothes back on to come out here for...I don't know."

"Larry, is it possible she might have been murdered?"

"We need to just wait and let the authorities handle it. Not much point in speculating."

When they reached the boardwalk leading to the parking lot, Larry tried his phone again. This time he was able to connect. Putting his phone away, he said, "We're supposed to wait in the parking lot—they'll contact the ranger."

They waited a seemingly long ten minutes, sipping water in the baking sun and not talking. A brown DNR pickup raced into the parking lot and screeched to a stop.

A very young, very tall skinny man emerged. Frannie's first impression was of the kids she had taught in junior high. How depressing that authority figures keep getting younger.

Larry offered his hand to the ranger.

"I'm Larry Shoemaker—we spoke briefly last night. I'm the one who called."

"Brayton Phillips—the head ranger," the young man replied. "You're the retired cop, right? I talked to so many people last night," he added almost apologetically. His face was flushed and he kept pulling at his collar. A death

31

in his park was obviously a new experience for him. "Um, this woman is at Bogg's Retreat? Were there others down there with you?"

"Yes, our friends, four of them. I asked them to wait and turn anyone else back."

The ranger wiped his brow with the back of his hand. "You wait here. I'll send them back. The county sheriff should be here in just a few minutes. If it's okay with him, you can go back to the campground but don't talk to anyone else. I will need to talk to Maeve's husband before he hears from someone else, you understand?" It's hard to look stern when you also look twelve.

He noticed a well-used blue Honda and peered inside. Frannie said, "That's Mrs. Schlumm's car, isn't it? I remember seeing it by their camper."

The ranger did not answer as he checked the doors. He was not going to share much with them. The car was not locked. A purse sat open in the front seat, contents spilled.

He left the car and hurried down the boardwalk that led to the trail.

THE REST OF THE GROUP had just arrived at the parking lot when a sheriff's car rolled in. A large man emerged with a trim woman, both in uniform.

Larry stepped forward. "I'm Larry Shoemaker, Sheriff. I made the 911 call."

"Sheriff Buzz Ingrham, and this is Deputy Linda Smith," the sheriff said. "In which cave did you find this woman?"

Larry pointed in the general direction. "Bogg's Retreat—one of the last ones on the left trail. The ranger is down there."

"I'm familiar with it. Linda, will you please get everyone's names and information? Then you can all return to the campground. Soon as the county doc gets here, we'll be up to talk to you further."

He also cautioned them against speaking to anyone else and headed down the trail. Deputy Smith pulled out a notebook and very quickly noted their names, home addresses, and camping sites. She was fortyish with thin lips and pinched features, but when she was done, she thanked them and smiled, transforming her face into a much warmer one.

"Please go back to your campsites and we'll be up to get your statements shortly." As she turned to leave, Donna touched her elbow. "Are we all suspects?" she demanded.

"Everyone will be interviewed, ma'am."

THEY TRUDGED BACK TO the campground, the dogs seeming as relieved to be back to the relative familiarity as the humans.

"I wonder why Dave hadn't reported his wife missing earlier this morning," Frannie said.

"Maybe he knew she was leaving and didn't expect her back yet. Or their home is near here and she goes home occasionally," Jane Ann said.

"Maybe he killed her!" Donna said. "He wasn't very happy with her last night."

Jane Ann frowned. "Based on that, we'd all be dead."

They fell into lawn chairs, all in some phase of shock.

"I'm going to have a smoke," Mickey announced, launching himself out of his chair and heading for his camper.

"Mickey!" Jane Ann said, turning to watch him rummage in one of the storage compartments. He produced a smashed pack and a lighter.

"I know, I know, this is my emergency stash. Just one. It isn't every day we find a body."

She sighed while Larry admonished him. "Mick, keep your voice down."

"Sorry." He sank down in his chair again.

Jane Ann picked up a magazine and leafed through with quick, unfocused glances at each page. When her husband laid the battered pack of cigarettes on the arm of his chair, she snatched them and stuck them in her pocket. "I'll take care of these." Mickey grimaced like a teenager losing his car keys.

Donna paced from the fire pit to the road peering in both directions and not seeing much. Rob fiddled with a radio, trying to tune in a local news station and Frannie just sat in a daze.

Larry ran his hand across his short gray stubble of hair, one hand on his hip. "Let's think about something else. What's on the menu for tonight? Are we cooking?"

Frannie perked up a little. "We have chicken marinating. Donna was going to make potato salad."

Donna turned around. "I did. I make amazing potato salad. And I think we have several salads left from last night."

"A little Encore Buffet," Jane Ann said. "And we never got to the apple cobbler last night."

"So we'll need a fire tonight. . .probably start it about 3:00, d'ya think? We should have good coals by 5:00 then," Larry said.

Just then Ranger Phillips pulled up in his truck. When he noticed Stub and his friends packing up, he rolled down his passenger window motioning them over. The group could not hear what was being said, but they could guess and it was obvious that the news that the men had to stay put for the time being was not well received.

The ranger then drove on down the road toward the host camper. Stub headed across the road toward them. "What's going on? He told us we can't leave! We have a site reserved in Nebraska tonight that we've already paid for. What's happening?" The night before, Stub had maintained amazing equanimity in the face of all his mishaps, but it seemed his buddies were getting fed up and he was taking the brunt of it.

"We aren't supposed to talk about it. I think the sheriff will be here soon and explain everything," Larry said.

"Sheriff! But what—?" he stopped as he noticed Larry shaking his head. "Some kind of terrorist alert or—" He

35

trailed off and gave up, returning to his friends. They gathered around receiving only a shake of the head, and shot questioning, even angry, glances over at Larry.

Trying to lighten things up Mickey said, "Well. Is it time for lunch yet?"

"Didn't you guys tell us your camping trips were always so relaxing?" Rob said.

Frannie took charge. "It's not lunch time, but I'm going to make another pot of coffee and we have muffins left. We might as well cool it now, because sounds like there are no other options until the sheriff gets here." She carried the drained pot into the camper.

Larry followed her in. "You've been pretty quiet. Are you okay?"

"Yeah, it's just...." She stopped and set the pot she was filling in the sink and turned to face him. "Without even seeing her, it reminds me of Mom."

Larry looked at her, puzzled. "I can't say I knew Maeve well, but in no way did she remind me of your mother."

"I know, except that she's gone and it makes no sense. Do you suppose she has—had—kids?" Now she was unable to hold back tears, not sobs, just soft grief.

He put his arms around her. "I'm sure we will know before long." They stayed that way a minute, and then she turned back to the sink, splashed her face and finished the coffee. A couple of deep breaths helped and she took the pot back outside and plugged it in.

They gathered around the picnic table, mugs and water bottles in hand. Jane Ann had cut up more fruit and everyone helped themselves to a second breakfast. Frannie watched her sister-in-law organize the table, already feeling wilted and dowdy. Jane Ann looked fresh and crisp in the same simple khaki capris and white blouse she had started out in that morning. It wasn't fair. Good thing she liked Jane Ann.

"Boy, the atmosphere is really oppressive, in more ways than one," Mickey said.

Rob said, "I wonder when they'll let us leave the park."

"Yeah, there's that winery that we wanted to check out this afternoon," Donna said. "I bet the tasting room is air-conditioned."

Larry shook his head. "Unless they determine Maeve's death was an accident, I don't expect we'll be going anywhere soon. You might have to plan on turning the air on in your camper and taking a nap instead."

Mickey was their semi-official weather watcher. "The good news is it's supposed to be much nicer tomorrow, cooler and lower humidity. The bad news is there's a storm warning out later tonight as the front moves through."

"Wouldn't want a boring night, now would we?" Frannie said.

The talk returned to Maeve's death. "Still can't imagine what she was doing out there," Donna said.

"There was a flashlight on the floor of the cave," Jane Ann said, "So maybe she was out there in the middle of the night."

Rob said, "Even if she went on an early morning hike, she may have had a flashlight along to see in the caves."

Frannie shook her head. "I've been thinking about that. I sat out here with my coffee from just after sunup. I never saw her car or her go by. I took Cuba for a walk early but I didn't go by their camper. Donna, did you see her car when you took Buster out?"

Donna sat forward. "No! But I wasn't really looking," she said. She looked disappointed to have missed an exclusive piece of information — and probably the attention that would bring.

Mickey said, "Here comes the fuzz, here comes the fuzz…". Larry gave him a look.

Sheriff Ingrham and Deputy Smith had parked their patrol car in the road and were getting out. They looked around at the immediate campsites and spotted the Shoemakers and their friends at the picnic table.

The sheriff smiled rather grimly as they approached. "Handy to find you all in one spot,"

Frannie jumped up to pull up some lawn chairs. "Do you want to talk to us all together?"

"That'll be fine for now."

"Coffee?" Jane Ann asked. The sheriff shook his head and held up his bottled water but Linda Smith nodded.

"That would be great."

The sheriff leaned back in the lawn chair at a dangerous tilt and Deputy Smith pulled out a notebook and pen.

"Tell me how you happened to come upon Mrs. Schlumm's body," he said, nodding at Larry.

"We were just hiking the trail. The caves, as you know, are closed, but we wanted to get a hike in before it got too hot. We were trying to look inside from that area below the entrance when one of our dogs, Buster, suddenly picked up the scent and ran up to the entrance. Before we could get him pulled back, he knocked over a couple of rocks that were covering the foot."

"Was the dog on a leash?"

"Yes."

"Who all actually went into the cave?"

"I did at first," Larry said. "I had a small flashlight and could see that her condition didn't look very hopeful. I asked my sister, Jane Ann—she's a nurse—to come up and check for vital signs. There was nothing. No one else came in. We tried to not touch anything more than necessary."

"How did you know Mrs. Schlumm?"

"We didn't really," Donna jumped in. "We just saw her around the campground last night. She had a couple of run-ins with other campers—she was kind of crabby—oof!" Rob had kicked his wife under the table.

"He asked Larry," he said quietly.

"Sorry," Donna said. Ingrham nodded, and if he was perturbed, hid it well.

"Ms....Ferraro?" The sheriff said looking at the notes Linda had taken earlier. "What is your medical training and experience?"

"I have a BS from the University of Iowa and was an ER and a surgical nurse for 27 years. I also worked as a school nurse for a couple of years."

"And what checks did you make on Mrs. Schlumm?"

"Well, I have to say after seeing the injury to her head, I wasn't hopeful. I called her name but got no response and I didn't find a pulse or sign of breathing."

"Did either of you see anything in the cave besides Mrs. Schlumm's body?"

Larry and Jane Ann both shook their heads and then Larry said, "Wait! There was a small flashlight on the floor of the cave. I didn't pick it up and look at it."

The sheriff nodded. "So that wasn't yours?"

Larry pulled his out of his pocket. "No, this is mine."

"Well, a deputy is checking for fingerprints now. Our equipment isn't sufficient to get anything off the rocks, but he will fingerprint that light."

Donna interrupted again. "Was it an accident, Sheriff? Or did someone. . ." She trailed off, unable to voice their worst fears.

"We don't know yet. It appears the injury to her head was caused by collision with a rock, but we don't know whether she fell or was hit. Until we know, we will treat it as a suspicious death." He turned to the whole group. "Since this is a state park, the DCI — Division of Criminal Investigation — is sending someone who should be here by afternoon. Until they give the word, the park is closed and everyone in the campground must remain here."

CHAPTER FIVE

LATE SATURDAY MORNING

RANGER PHILLIPS WALKED INTO the campsite and motioned the sheriff over. They conferred a minute and then the sheriff called Larry over.

"Phillips talked to Dave Schlumm who apparently just got up. He's called his daughter but she lives about an hour away and will be here as soon as she can. Meanwhile, we're pretty shorthanded and need to talk to everyone in the campground and set up a roadblock at the park entrance. I'm wondering if you would be willing to give us a hand? I'd like to have you and possibly your wife go sit with Dave until the daughter gets here."

Larry stuck his hands in his back pockets and hesitated before he answered. "I certainly can. I don't know about Frannie. She's taking this kind of hard."

The sheriff narrowed his eyes. "Did she know the deceased?"

"No, it's just that she lost her mother a couple of weeks ago and it's still pretty fresh. I'll ask her but I won't push her."

"Well, either way, we don't want Dave alone for a number of reasons. I'm hoping I can count on your discretion."

Larry nodded and walked back to his wife. When he explained the situation, she agreed to go and, in the time-honored custom of dealing with grief, suggested they take a thermos of coffee and the last of the muffins.

When they reached the Schlumms' trailer, Larry knocked lightly on the screen door and called inside at the same time.

They heard a shuffling step. Dave Schlumm appeared and opened the door without a word, his thick white mane more disheveled than the night before. He didn't speak but rather waited for them to do so.

"Mr. Schlumm, I'm Larry Shoemaker. We're camping here and the sheriff asked if we would come and keep you company until your daughter gets here," Larry said. Schlumm still didn't utter a word, but held the door open for them. He motioned them to the couch and sat down himself in a plush swivel rocker. The interior was neat and uncluttered with just a few family photos around. The windows were all open, but only warm, sticky air was coming in. They sat for a minute in silence.

"We also brought some coffee and some muffins," Frannie said. "Would you like some?"

He sat forward in the chair, elbows on knees, head hanging down. "Jus' coffee," he said but made no move. Frannie spotted a mug tree on the counter and poured him a cup from the thermos. The counter was spotless, as was the rest of the camper. Maeve, or perhaps Dave, was an excellent housekeeper.

She handed him the steaming mug and he barely raised his eyes to acknowledge her gesture.

"We're very sorry for your loss. It must be a terrible shock," Frannie said gently, thinking: duh, how original. He barely nodded, not looking up again.

Larry cleared his throat. "Mr. Schlumm, we were the ones who found your wife." Schlumm did look up at them now with small interest.

"Do you know why your wife was out there?" Frannie asked, ignoring her husband's slight frown.

Schlumm just shrugged and made a sound between a gulp and a sob. "Don't know."

Frannie changed the subject. "So your daughter lives nearby?"

He brightened. "Jodi. Yeah. About an hour away. Worried about her driving alone. She and her mom were so close. Maybe my grandson will drive her—her husband's gone on business."

"Do you have other children, Mr. Schlumm?" Frannie said.

"A boy. He lives in North Carolina. Gonna have Jodi call him. Just can't do it. Ranger called Jodi for me." He took a deep breath and continued. "Maeve, you know, was such a caring person." Not a side Frannie had noticed. "But it just upset her so when people didn't take care of things or broke the rules in the park. She loved this place."

"I'm sure she did. Are you sure you don't want a little bite to eat?"

"In a bit. Couldn't swallow anything solid right now."

Another silence. "How many grandchildren do you have, Mr. Schlumm?" Larry asked.

Again Dave Schlumm perked up. "Dave, please. No one calls me 'Mister'. Three. Jodi's boy, Aaron, is 19, and Darren, our son, has two daughters, 8 and 10. That's them in that photo." He pointed at the end table next to Larry. Larry picked it up and held it so Frannie could see it too.

"Good looking kids," Larry said.

Frannie agreed. "They certainly are. Do you get to see them often?"

"Aaron we do, being close by. The girls not so often. Always come in the summer for a couple weeks, though. They loved staying in the park with us. That upset Maeve too. Supposed to come the end of this month but now we're leaving. . ." He stopped and looked up. He'd forgotten for a moment that leaving the park was not the worst thing facing him now.

Frannie said, "Mr. Schlumm—Dave—would you mind if I used your bathroom? Or I could just go to the shower house."

"No, no—go ahead. It's on the right. Can't get lost." He gave a very small, sad smile.

"Thanks."

In the tiny bathroom, Frannie noticed a jumble of bottles on the little counter, including an empty aspirin bottle on its side. She had to remove the bottle cap from the sink to wash her hands. Not in keeping with the rest of what she had seen in the camper.

When she returned to the living area, Dave said "Sorry about the mess in there. Maeve doesn't usually

44

leave things like that. Better get it picked up before Jodi gets here."

"Does — did — Maeve have health problems?" Frannie asked.

"Nah, healthy as a horse most times. She's had headaches more often lately. Stress, I guess. Why?"

"There's an empty aspirin bottle on the counter. Could she have gone out for more last night? Is there any place open late?"

Dave sat up straight. "Don't know. Possible. There's a 24-hour shop over on the highway."

"Her purse was in the car," Frannie said, looking at Larry. He frowned at her interrogating and she quickly glanced away.

They heard voices outside, and a tall shape was silhouetted against the screen door. Dave stood and put his hand on the door.

"Ralph. Good of you to come," he opened the door.

Larry also stood. "We'll wait outside."

"No, let's all go outside. Getting stuffy in here." A champion understatement, Frannie thought. "This is Ralph Bonnard, the local funeral director. Uh, sorry, your names slipped my mind."

"Larry Shoemaker and my wife Frannie."

They shook hands. Dave continued, "Sheriff asked them to sit with me until Jodi gets here. Kinda hard to take it all in."

They all trooped outside. They noticed then that Ralph Bonnard was not alone. A tall, broad-shouldered young man with short blond hair and Paul Newman blue eyes stood to the side. Both Bonnard and the young man wore suits, crisp white shirts and dark ties.

"Dave," Bonnard said, "I don't believe you've met my new assistant, Joel Marner. He's from Chicago and just been here a month or two." Marner shook hands with Dave and nodded at the other two. "First we want to express our deepest condolences. This is never easy, but even harder in these circumstances. The sheriff asked us to come out here because they aren't letting anyone leave the park at this time. But as you know, both of you have preplanned arrangements so there won't be many decisions for you."

Larry said, "Excuse me. This should be a private discussion. We'll go back to our campsite, number 17, and if you leave before Dave's daughter gets here, stop and let us know and we'll come back."

Bonnard nodded and shook Larry's hand again. The Shoemakers walked away.

When they were away from Schlumm's camper, Frannie said "Creepy."

"What? The mortician? The arrangements?"

"No, that assistant. He seemed to be staring at us the whole time. You'd think he would be concentrating on the client."

"I didn't notice. But he's new—and young. Probably wondered why complete strangers would be there. I mean, that was obvious because Schlumm couldn't remember our names to introduce us."

"Could be."

Along the road in every site people milled around or sat speaking quietly. No one was out on the road. Normally, in the daylight hours, any campground road was a racetrack for bicycles and skateboards. Kids capitalized on the infrequent traffic and safe surroundings, speeding from one end to the other in a continual chase. But today, that safety was in question and the same kids slouched in lawn chairs drawing circles in the dirt with sticks or poking their siblings with the same.

As they neared their own site, they noticed their visitor from the night before, River, hanging on the back of a woman's chair. She appeared to be in her thirties. Her shoulder length dark blond hair flopped forward over her face as she tried to read a paperback and ignore the bouncing accessory on the back of her chair. In concession to the heat, she put her hand under the back of her hair and pushed it up on top of her head. Just then, River spotted them.

"Hey! Can I come play with your dog?"

His mother, assuming that's who she was, snapped "No! You're staying right here." Then she looked a little sheepish and said to them "Sorry. He better stay here."

"We understand," said Frannie. "Maybe later, okay, River?"

His face fell but he nodded and resumed trying to annoy his mother.

The Nowaks and the Ferraros were still at the picnic table but the sheriff and deputy had moved on to other campers. Mickey looked up from a day old crossword.

"Hey! You're back."

"He's so observant," Frannie said to Larry.

"Yeah, yeah. How's Schlumm doing?"

Larry took a seat. "He seems in shock, no surprise. The funeral director came so we took our leave. Schlumm's daughter is supposed to be here soon. How much longer did the sheriff stay?"

"He left right after you did. Went over to the guys across the road and was there quite a while. Actually, he just moved on."

"He asked about that box," Donna reminded him.

"Oh, yeah, he wanted to know if any of us had seen a container of some sort near those boulders. We told him again that you and Jane Ann were the only ones who went into the cave."

"It had rounded corners," Donna couldn't wait to add. "They found an imprint in the dirt. He said he'd be back to talk to you about it."

"Well, there wasn't anything when we were there," Larry said.

"And if there had been, it couldn't have disappeared unless we took it," Rob said. "No one was there after us except the sheriff."

"The ranger was," Frannie said.

Larry held up his hands. "Take it easy. Let's not jump to conclusions…"

He was interrupted by Stub coming up behind him. The big man took a seat at the end of the table, causing it to tip slightly.

"Wow, a murder, huh? And you guys found her?"

"As far as we know, they haven't decided if it was an accident or not," Larry said.

Stub gave a crooked smile. "Well, if it was a murder, there's probably no shortage of suspects."

Frannie thought it was time to derail him. "So what are you guys going to do about your reservation for tonight? Even if the DCI says this afternoon that we can leave the park, you'll never get that far tonight, not unless you want to set up in the dark." She thought that they had enough trouble in the daylight.

"Big change of plans," Stub said. "We had to reserve three nights here anyway, 'cause of the holiday weekend so we're just going to stay here until Monday." He laughed briefly. "Not much choice, eh? The only other reservation we had made was the one for Nebraska—we were just going to follow the sun, y'know what I mean? But even I have to admit we probably bit off a little too much. So Monday we'll go back to the Chicago area and find someplace close to home we can hang out for the rest of the time." He lowered his voice and seemed to expect his next words to be a shocker to them, "Guys are kind of fed up with me, I think, even though none of them wanted to take responsibility for organizing anything. Oddest thing is that Randy is the only one who wanted to keep going, and I didn't think he was having a good time."

"Sounds like a good idea—going back, I mean," Mickey said. "We usually go somewhere near home at the first of every season to make sure everything's working even though we've been camping for years."

Stub looked up as a car came slowly through the campground, driven by a fairly young woman.

"Huh! I haven't seen her around here and I didn't think they were letting anyone else in."

"Might be Mr. Schlumm's daughter. She is coming to stay with him," Larry said.

"Schlumm? Oh, is that the guy's name? Even though his wife had plenty to say to us last night, never did introduce herself. Are most of the hosts in these campgrounds that grouchy? Don't they get paid to be more helpful?"

"Actually, they don't get paid at all in most of the state and county parks," Larry said. "They get free camping and that's it. Most of the hosts are pretty low profile but we've had some great ones."

Mickey said, "We were at a small county park once where there weren't very many campers and the hosts cooked us a prime rib in cast iron over the coals. It was fabulous! Remember that place?" He looked at the others.

"That was some meal," Frannie said. "The guy loved cast iron cooking and did it just for the fun of it. He completely covered the meat in rock salt and it was wonderful. We provided the rest of the meal."

"Really? A prime rib?" Stub said.

Jane Ann added, "Actually, the hosts are supposed to just handle the reservations and answer questions about the park and local attractions. In reality, they can get stuck with cleaning up messes and other problems."

Stub heaved himself up from the table. "Well, I'd better go help unpack some stuff. We didn't get most of it out since we were just going to be here overnight. Have to scare up something to fix for supper tonight. Probably won't be getting any prime rib here tonight and I don't supposed we'll be able to get pizza delivered. What do you guys do for fun anyway, I mean if you can't go anywhere?"

"We've never had a situation like this before," Mickey said. "But we always have cards and games, plus we all like to read. TV reception often isn't very good in state parks. No cable and all the trees. If you need cards, you're welcome to borrow some."

Stub thanked them and said goodbye, lumbering back across the road.

As they began pulling out the makings for lunch, a car pulled over and Frannie recognized the funeral director and his assistant. She walked over and the assistant rolled down his window. Ralph Bonnard leaned over from the driver's side.

"Dave Schlumm's daughter Jodi arrived a little while ago, so you won't need to go back."

"I think we saw her go by," Frannie said. "How is Dave doing?"

Bonnard shrugged. "Not much change. They were going to call his son next and I think he's worried about that—you know, it's very hard to give the news to family."

"Will they have services soon?"

"No, she wanted to be cremated and have her ashes scattered here at the park. They'll do that and have a memorial service sometime later." Frannie noticed that the young assistant got a little smirk on his face before quickly covering it up. He studied the campsite where Stub and his friends appeared to be discussing the situation.

"Okay. Thank you." She backed away, baffled by the young man's reaction, and watched the car continue slowly down the road. She returned to the picnic table where Larry, Donna, and Mickey were laying out sandwich makings and condiments along with corn salad from the night before.

"What was that about?" Larry asked.

"Oh, that funeral director is just letting us know that Dave's daughter was here and we didn't need to return." She shook her head slightly. "That assistant, though, really freaks me out—I would swear he was delighted at the prospect of cremating Maeve Schlumm."

"I think someone's letting their imagination go a little loosey goosey," Larry said in a singsong canter.

"Maybe he's a body snatcher," Donna said.

Frannie gave them her most disgusted look. "Grow up, both of you," she said.

Lunch was light since they had been snacking on muffins and fruit all morning. Jane Ann produced some of her famous oatmeal craisin cookies as dessert and reported that while she was in their RV, their daughter Justine had called.

"She was almost frantic," she said, a little trace of pleasure escaping at her daughter's concern. "Their birth mother's current husband—second, I think—is a county dispatcher and relayed the news to them. She thought they ought to drive over and 'be with us.' I assured them we are well protected."

Mickey harrumphed and put his arm around her shoulders. "I can't believe they would question your safety." She leaned her head against him, contented, and started to respond, but he grinned and said, "I mean, Larry's here." She punched him playfully in the gut.

CHAPTER SIX

AFTER THEY CLEARED LUNCH away, Donna took Larry's advice and headed back to her camper for a nap. Jane Ann, a closet artist, got out her sketchpad and settled in her camp chair with a glass of iced tea. Larry tuned in a baseball game on his radio, stretched out in a lounger, and promptly fell asleep. Frannie, Mickey and Rob all opted for their books. The heat seemed to be suppressing all sound. Quiet murmurs came from the sites around them and blended with the buzzing of insects. Only the canopy of shade made the day bearable.

The only activity was across the road as the Chicago guys pulled more coolers and boxes from the RV storage compartments and piled them by their campsite. Occasionally a family would stroll by, children kept close, on their way to the shower house or other campsites. For Frannie, even though the death itself was a big shock, the realization that such a threat could exist in a situation always perceived before as benign was the most difficult concept to grasp.

The arrival of the sheriff's car broke into the illusory peacefulness. The sheriff's passenger was not Deputy Smith. A short, stocky, dark-haired man emerged from the car and together they approached the Shoemakers and their fellow campers. Larry woke with a start and tried to act like he hadn't been asleep.

"Folks, this is Warren Sanchez, an agent for the State Division of Criminal Investigation. He would like to hear your story again and maybe ask a couple of other questions."

Sanchez wore dress slacks and a polo shirt open at the neck. He frequently swiped his hair back off his forehead, smiled easily, and shook hands all around. Iced water and tea were offered and accepted. They all settled in the circle of chairs; Donna's absence was explained and excused.

Agent Sanchez leaned forward in his chair, and keeping his voice low, said, "I'd like to start with last night. I understand you witnessed several—what? confrontations?—involving the victim. Did you know her previously?"

They all shook their heads. Larry said, "We've camped here before but not this year and the hosts often change."

"Well, tell me about these confrontations."

Larry described the difficulties Stub's group had experienced and Maeve's reaction. The agent looked over at the campsite in question and the others followed suit. Randy and another man sat on coolers, looking over their shoulders at them, not happy. Stub stood holding a lawn chair and in serious discussion with another of the group. Everyone on both sides quickly lowered their eyes or stared elsewhere, embarrassed to be caught looking.

Rob then explained his lighting and music setup, going into way more detail than anyone wanted to hear.

Agent Sanchez, however, sat patiently listening. When Rob finished, he asked, "Did you argue with her?"

"No! Well, I said I didn't think it was quiet hours yet. Actually, I was going to turn it down after my friends had a chance to adequately admire it." Rob gave a sly smile. "She said it was inappropriate at any time. Then she really got mad when the guys next door defended me. She really didn't like them."

"Were there any other incidents?"

"Those bikers," Mickey said.

Larry explained. "We don't know what happened between them, but we saw Mrs. Schlumm head over that way after they passed and she didn't look happy. The bikes were noisy but it wasn't 10:00 yet."

"Okay, we'll be talking to them later. On your hike, did you meet anyone else on the trail?"

They all looked at each other and shook their heads. "It was still pretty early," Mickey said. "We wanted to beat the heat."

"One other question, did any of you see a box or container in the cave when you were there—or remove anything like that?"

Again Larry took the lead. "My sister and I were the only ones who went in the cave. There wasn't anything else that we noticed except a small flashlight."

Agent Sanchez said, "The sheriff found that and it appears to have belonged to Maeve Schlumm. Only her fingerprints were on it."

"How do you know something else was there?" Frannie asked.

"Marks in the dust show something was dragged across the floor of the cave and then left near the boulders. Something rectangular with rounded corners."

Frannie thought a minute. "What about a cooler?"

"We thought about that, but coolers have pretty deep curves on the corners. These were just barely rounded—maybe even a cardboard box with the corners kind of bashed in."

Sheriff Ingrham leaned forward and cleared his throat. "Have any of you seen the people staying in that silver camper down the road?"

"They were there last night—I think all evening," Mickey said.

Frannie spoke up. "I saw the red pickup leave early this morning when I first came out. Maybe about 6:00. I didn't see who was in it and haven't seen anyone around since."

"No one else has either. Guess I'll need to get contact information from Ranger Phillips. How about the people next door? Have you seen a man around that campsite?"

Jane Ann said, "Just a little boy and I assume his mom. I don't think we've seen anyone else." She looked at the others and they all shook their heads. "The boy, River, was over here last night and mentioned his dad but we haven't seen him."

"They're separated," the sheriff explained. "He's got a long history of drug use and dealing; the wife finally threw him out. 'Course we have a roadblock up at the park entrances but if you do see anyone new around there, let us know right away."

Agent Sanchez rose to leave and the sheriff followed.

"Agent, have they decided yet whether it was an accident or not?" Larry asked.

"Not definitely. But we don't believe it was an accident. We found a large rock down by the stream with some blood on it. Most had washed off, but if it matches Mrs. Schlumm, it's unlikely that it rolled down to that particular spot."

Mickey said, "I'm surprised you've been able to keep this from the media."

"Oh, we haven't," the agent said. "We're handling the situation at the entrances. Two of the area TV stations have been here, as well as a couple of newspaper reporters. I'm sure it's on the Net by now, too."

"Do you have a time of death yet?"

"Apparently around 2:00 a.m. And we don't know yet why she was out there at that time."

"My wife might have some insight into that question," Larry said, nodding at Frannie. Agent Sanchez cocked his head at her.

Frannie hesitated a few seconds; she'd had the impression that Larry didn't like her 'meddling.' Now he urged her on.

"We spent a little time with Mr. Schlumm waiting for his daughter to arrive. The sheriff asked us to." She looked to the sheriff for confirmation and he nodded. "I found an open, empty aspirin bottle on the bathroom counter, and when I asked Mr. Schlumm about it, he said his wife had been having pretty severe headaches lately. She might have gone for more aspirin. I mean, I asked him if that was a possibility and he said there's an all-night convenience store nearby. So he agreed she might have done that."

The agent addressed Sheriff Ingrham. "Did Schlumm tell you anything about that?"

The sheriff shook his head. "He didn't say much at all. I don't put a lot of stock in what Dave says. We've had a domestic disturbance call or two on him before."

Larry was trying to stay professional and not interfere, but without thinking he asked, "You mean Dave abused his wife?"

"We'd rather not get into that," Agent Sanchez said, giving the sheriff a warning glance. "For the time being, the park is still closed. We are in the process of doing background checks on everyone here, although we have already verified Mr. Shoemaker's credentials since we may need to call on him more. In the meantime, I urge you all to be careful. Stay where there's people and don't go out at night alone."

They all stood around for a minute, lost in that sobering thought after the sheriff and DCI agent left.

"Well!" Rob said. "I guess he's just trying to lighten the mood and help us enjoy our weekend."

"Sounds like Maeve's murderer might have been pretty close to home," Jane Ann said.

"Right." Mickey rummaged his pockets.

"I have your smokes and you don't get them back."

Frannie said, "I don't know. His grief seemed pretty genuine. What did you think, Larry?"

"It might be genuine. It might be remorse. I've seen people react in a wide range of ways, guilty or not. Maybe he's even wondering if his wife was involved in something he didn't know about. There are lots of possibilities. The main thing we need to remember is to be careful."

Mickey said, "Yeah, there's more than one questionable character here this weekend. I like it better when we don't know anyone's secrets in the campground."

They all returned to their chairs and tried to pick up where they left off.

Frannie looked over Jane Ann's shoulder at the pencil sketch she had been working on. The Chicago boys' rented RV was in the background, indistinct and incomplete, while in the foreground was the jumble of coolers and equipment that had been pulled out that day, drawn in great detail.

"Wow, Jane Ann, I love the shading—you've really captured the shadows and light around that site. Such interesting shapes, too."

"Yeah, I'm pretty pleased, but now they've moved everything. And the light has changed too."

Frannie looked across the road and saw that many of the coolers and boxes had indeed been shifted around the campsite, some opened and contents pulled out.

"I can go ask them to put them all back just like it was," Frannie said.

"Right. I'm sure they'd be delighted. They've loaded and unloaded that stuff more than we do in a whole summer." Jane Ann laughed.

Frannie straightened up. "I'm in the mood for some totally pointless activity so I think I'll go take a shower. I skipped it this morning since we were going to hike. Give me a few minutes today of feeling semi-clean."

"Don't go home with any strangers," Mickey said.

She climbed the steps to the trailer and retrieved shower wash, shampoo, a hair brush and some clean clothes and rolled them all into a towel. As she walked toward the shower house, she observed the activity or lack thereof in the sites she passed. River and his mother were at the table with sandwiches and cheese curls. A small, older popup sat behind a battered blue pickup. A large thicket of shrubs and trees separated their campsite from the next. There a retirement age couple played cribbage at their picnic table. They waved and smiled and she waved and smiled back. On the other side of the road was a playground with a sand surface and basic equipment. Several younger children played there, all under the watchful eye of hot, tired-looking adults.

The playground and the shower house were situated on her right on the outside curve of a bend in the road. The bikers had the first campsite on the left after the curve and Agent Sanchez was talking to the two couples. The sheriff stood at the next site with another family, two young children clinging to their parents' legs and hiding their faces from the man in uniform. An older boy performed gymnastics on his skateboard right in front of the site, staying in earshot. Campers in sites on down the road stood or sat watching the questioning, waiting their turns under the spotlight of authority.

Dave Schlumm's camper, on the other side of the shower house, was all closed up with the air conditioner on top bravely and loudly trying to beat the heat.

When Frannie entered the women's side of the shower house, it was empty. Not a popular time of day for showers. She chose the cleanest looking stall and put her flip-flops on the slatted wooden bench. In these older facilities, sometimes the biggest challenge was to keep your fresh clothes and towel dry. One wall hook offered the only other perch for such items besides the bench. The shower itself consisted of a very small nozzle operated by a chain, which had to be held down with one hand to keep the water flowing. It worked adequately as long as you remembered to open your shower wash and shampoo before you started.

After finishing, she dressed and tried to keep her clothes out of the water on the floor. The outside door opened and someone came in. She felt a brief moment of panic, but soon after heard water running in the sink, the footsteps receding and the door shutting again. She let out a breath she didn't even realize she was holding.

She sometimes used the hand dryer to dry her hair but the hot air didn't have much appeal today and she admitted to herself that she was anxious to get back out in the open. She took her bundle, exited the building, and sat on a wooden bench by the back corner of the building in the shade. She had a view of the playground and could brush some of the dampness out of her hair. In the peaceful setting, performing a simple, repetitive task, she could almost forget the questions and turmoil disrupting this weekend.

That is, it was peaceful for a few minutes until she became aware of sounds coming from the backside of the building. The beeps of someone dialing a cell phone prefaced a low voice in almost a stage whisper. She froze and although she would normally move out of range to give the caller privacy, the odd circumstances kept her in her seat.

"Hey, it's me again. Don't know what to do. (Pause) I know, but we can't leave. Cops have the park closed. (Pause) I don't think I can make this delivery…(Pause) Well, you're going to have to work something else out. (Pause) Just text, don't call." With no sign off, the phone slammed shut. Frannie quickly gathered her things and headed to the road. She wondered if someone watched her but when she looked back, saw no one. She considered reporting the call to the agent or the sheriff but didn't see either of them right then and didn't want to hang around.

Back at the campsite, Larry was sorting through his tote of outdoor supplies. He looked up. "Hi Babe. Feel better?"

"A little." She hung her towel on the detachable clothesline on the rear of the trailer and carried the rest of her stuff inside. When she came back out, she said to Larry, "Go for a little walk with me?"

"Sure. I was just getting stuff out for the fire. Time to start it pretty soon."

Cuba raised her head to check on their plans, but decided they must be crazy to go for a walk and dropped back on her paws and closed her eyes.

"She's smarter than us. She's better off staying in the shade," Larry said. They went the opposite direction from the shower house toward the parking lot and trailhead. When they were away from most of the campers, Frannie told Larry about the phone call she'd just overheard.

"Did the guy see you?" Larry asked with heightened concern.

"I don't think so. He was around the corner of the building."

"Could you tell who it was?"

"No, he kept his voice low. But we haven't talked to any of the men here much except Stub and I don't think it was him."

"What about Dave Schlumm?"

"Oh yeah...well again, I don't think so but it's possible. Sounded younger than him though. Do you think it's connected to Maeve's death?"

"Hard to say. The word 'delivery'—you're sure that's what he said?" She nodded. "Could be something legitimate, I suppose, but telling the other person to text and not call makes it sound like it's not. Of course, anyone here could be involved in some kind of illegal pickup or delivery totally unrelated to Maeve's death, and because none of us can leave, has to make a change in plans. We'll have to pass this on to Agent Sanchez. Drugs are the first thing that comes to mind."

"I know," she agreed. They had reached the parking lot. "Let's turn back." They reversed their direction and as they did so Larry draped his arm across her shoulders. It was reassuring, even though her recently fresh, bright aqua camp shirt was already starting to stick to her back.

"Well, until this is over, I don't even want you going to the shower house alone, Frannie. Whatever this guy is up to, if he caught even a glimpse of you, there could be a risk."

"Okay." She pushed damp hair away from her face. "This heat is making the whole thing worse. It's like the weather is helping to keep us penned in."

"I just heard a report on the weather radio while you were gone. They're still talking storms tonight, possibly severe, and then better tomorrow. Like Mickey says, good news, bad news."

They trudged up the road in silence for a few minutes, flies buzzing around them in the stillness.

"What's your take on this, Larry? Do you think it was someone in the campground? Or totally unconnected?" Frannie asked.

"She definitely annoyed a lot of people but hardly a cause for murder."

"And who would have known she was even out there at that hour?"

"They could have seen her go by in the car."

"Yes, but for someone to follow, catch up to her, and get her to stop—it just doesn't fit time-wise. Did Stub and his buddies see anything? They were up late."

"The sheriff says they claim not. They say they went to bed about 1:00."

Frannie remembered something. "Mickey said he saw at least some of them out by their fire around 1:30."

"You're right. But they did say around 1:00. People usually don't know what time they did something exactly. I think most likely she surprised someone doing something they weren't supposed to—something with consequences worth killing for. I imagine the remoteness of a place like a state park attracts quite a few unsavory transactions."

"But the parks all close at 10:30."

"Technically they do, and the gates are closed at the entrances but that wouldn't prevent anyone from walking in."

"Well, then, if she did happen on a drug sale or something like that, it could have been the guy on the phone or it could have been a local just using a drop site."

"You're right," he conceded. They seemed to be going in figurative circles as they plodded straight ahead on the road.

At the entrance to the campground, they found the sheriff and Agent Sanchez in the patrol car, AC running, talking and checking notes. Larry tapped on the agent's window.

The window glided down silently and the agent smiled slightly as he recognized Larry.

"Yes, Mr. Shoemaker?"

"Frannie overheard a phone conversation a little bit ago that you should know about."

Frannie described the call and the voice again for the agent.

"And you didn't recognize the voice or see anyone?"

"No. It was definitely a man and he tried to keep his voice as low as possible."

The agent finished his notes and smiled up at her. "Thank you. This could be very important. It may not have anything to do with Mrs. Schlumm's death but it definitely sounds like something's up." The smile disappeared. "I caution you again to be careful, Mrs. Shoemaker, and let us handle this."

CHAPTER SEVEN

WHEN THEY GOT BACK to the campsite, Mickey and Rob were walking around making half-hearted motions toward starting a fire. Some wood was piled by the fire ring and Mickey had gotten out a fire starter.

"You were leaving us with all the fire starting responsibility, weren't you? Don't you want any supper?" Mickey asked.

"Right. Like you've never started any fires?" Larry said.

"I didn't say I couldn't. But I had to get out of my chair… ."

"There's the problem—your lazy butt."

The 'I can top you' insults between the brothers-in-law had been going on for forty years. Frannie and Jane Ann didn't expect it to end anytime soon. Still arguing, the men got a fire started and Mickey pulled a garbage bag out of a storage compartment containing an ingenious grill system. In less than five minutes a single pole rose next to the fire ring with a crosspiece holding a chain from which a round grill was suspended. The grill could be adjusted up or down and swung away from the fire to turn meat or leave the ring free for a larger campfire.

Rob sat forward in his lawn chair watching Mickey's every move. When the grill was complete, Rob sat back. "Wow. That is excellent. We used one of those tripods and it was nothing but trouble—tripped over it, burned my arm on it once trying to flip burgers—where'd you get that?"

"Some guy in the Quad Cities makes them in his garage. Larry's got one too."

"And you guys almost always cook over a fire, rather than a gas grill? Or charcoal?"

Mickey shrugged. "Usually."

Donna, risen from her nap and looking perkier than any of the others, admired the grill as well. "Anything new on Maeve Schlumm?" she asked.

"You missed a visit from the DCI agent and the sheriff because you're so lazy," Rob said.

Donna stuck out her tongue at him. "What'd they say?"

Rob sobered. "They think she was murdered. Wanted to know about all the arguments she had last night. Told us to stay put and stay safe."

Donna had no comment. Her eyes wandered around the surrounding campsites.

Rob said, "And the sheriff said Schlumm has been reported for abusing his wife."

Donna's eyes grew wide. "Really? That must be it, then. That would explain why she was out where she was. He must have chased her!"

Larry resisted rolling his eyes. "Donna, that may be the case but there's too much they don't know yet. It's best if we don't go around making accusations—just makes you into a target."

Frannie recognized Larry's attempt to diplomatically tell Donna to shut up. It seemed effective; Donna nodded seriously and gazed down the road to the Schlumm's camper. She moved her lawn chair closer into the circle, facing the road so she could keep watch.

One of the biker couples strolled by, checking out the grill and the group. Just past the site, they hesitated, and turned back. No leathers today; instead they wore shorts and denim shirts with the sleeves cut off, exposing some mean tattoos. The man held out his hand to Mickey, who sat closest to the road.

"Richard Evans. My wife, Elaine," with a backward toss of his head by way of introduction. "Are you the cop that found the body?"

"I'm Mickey—that would be my brother-in-law, Larry," Mickey pointed.

"Man. That's something. What a way to start your day, huh?" he said to Larry. Not very tall and built like a refrigerator, Richard carried his bulk in his arms and chest. Curly brown hair framed crinkled blue eyes and a big smile. Elaine, too, was sturdy and big shouldered without being fat. Her gray curly hair stopped just short of her shoulders and was pulled back from her face and behind her ears with barrettes. Both evidenced the outdoor life with tanned leathery skin.

Now Richard walked over by the grill, hands on hips. "This is what we stopped to check out. Very clever! How'd you come by this—or did you make it?"

Larry and Mickey took turns explaining about the grill. They almost could field a routine, they had been asked so many times. Rob offered Richard a beer, which he gratefully accepted and the extra lawn chairs were produced. Elaine scratched and cooed to both dogs — obviously a softy.

Larry said, "So, what do you do, Richard?"

"Yeah, I'm a chiropractor," Richard said.

"Seriously?" Mickey said. When Richard nodded, Mickey added, "That gives new meaning to the term 'adjustment.'"

Richard roared and slapped his knee. "You bet!"

"What about you, Elaine? Do you work? Rob and Donna are the only ones in our group who are still productive members of society," Frannie said.

Elaine gave a sweet smile. "I farm." Then seeing their surprised faces, she continued. "We inherited my parents' farm and I love working it. Richard has his practice in a small town about three miles from us. I'm strictly a grain farmer — no livestock — so it leaves us free to head out on our bikes on weekends. There really are great parks in this part of the state."

"I love your tents," Donna said. "Very minimalist!"

"You're welcome to check them out any time," Elaine said.

Richard brought the conversation back to the topic on all of their minds. "Yeah, I've seen the sheriff a couple of times and the agent talked to us a little bit ago. You think they really suspect someone in the campground of murder?"

"They have to consider that possibility," Larry, master of the non-answer, said.

"Looked like you guys had a run-in with Mrs. Schlumm last night too," Rob said.

Richard sighed. "Yeah, she reamed us out for noise. It wasn't 10:00 yet, though."

"She was already mad at us and those guys across the road," Rob explained. "Probably why she came down so hard on you."

"Yeah, but can't imagine that anyone killed her over that kind of thing. What about the husband? Isn't the husband always the most likely suspect?" Richard said.

"Is that a threat?" Elaine asked, getting a chuckle from everyone.

Frannie said. "His grief seems pretty sincere."

"People can be pretty good actors," Larry observed.

Mickey got up and checked the state of the fire. He carefully placed another log. They wanted fairly hot coals to cook their chicken. "Look at Larry. Some people actually think he's a professional cop."

Richard said to Larry, "I thought you were a retired cop." But then noticing the smirk on Mickey's face, he nodded with amused understanding.

Richard said, "Yeah, well, I hope they solve it soon. They can't keep us here forever…can they?"

"Not likely," Larry smiled. They discussed some of the other parks they liked, and then Richard heaved himself out of his chair.

"Hey, thanks for the beer. Stop by at our joint and we'll repay you."

"And we give free tours of our abode," Elaine said.

They talked about supper. They talked about supper a lot on their trips. What they were going to have, how to cook it, how hot the coals needed to be, what kind of dessert to finish it off with. But this trip they soon switched back to talking about Maeve's death.

"Maybe Richard's right—maybe it was Dave. He probably knows when she left the camper and he's not saying," Rob said.

"I asked the ranger this morning about their leaving," Donna said. "He said it was partly because of complaints about Maeve, but I bet it also has to do with the domestic abuse thing."

Larry shook his head. "That ranger's quite a gossip." Larry always preferred that such matters were left to the authorities.

"He's young—quite young—really very, very young," Frannie said. "This has to be a very unusual situation for a state park."

Larry acknowledged that and added, "I do think we all need to be careful. Apparently everyone here knows that we found the body. The murderer may suspect we found more than that—other evidence. Frannie, go ahead and tell them about the phone call. This is serious business and I don't want any of you thinking Dave is the only possible threat."

Frannie related the phone call she overheard. The other four all looked a little stunned.

"This is like TV," Donna said.

"No," Larry said. "This is real life. That's why I said this is serious business."

The brown DNR pickup rumbled slowly along the road, stopping at each campsite. When he got to them, Ranger Phillips leaned out the window.

"Sheriff is calling a meeting at 7:00 tonight in the picnic shelter for everyone in the campground. Some things he wants to go over with everyone at the same time."

Mickey raised his hand in acknowledgement and the rest nodded. Ranger Phillips nudged the pickup along to the next site.

"Well," Donna said. "Maybe we'll finally learn something."

Jane Ann asked, "Will that fire be ready to cook pretty soon? If we can eat around 5:00, we won't have to hurry and can clean up before the meeting."

Mickey looked at his watch. "That should work. We can put the chicken on in about half an hour. I'd better rest up." He flopped in his lawn chair.

Frannie wondered more than ever about Dave Schlumm. She had left their thermos that morning and it offered an excuse to meet his daughter and maybe find out a little more about the Schlumms' relationship. In spite of Richard's comment about the husband always being a likely suspect, she had a hard time believing that was the case here.

"I'm going over to Dave Schlumm's. I left our thermos with him this morning and I'll see how he's doing," she said.

"Whoa," Larry said. "After what we just learned about him? I'd better go."

Frannie counted off on her fingers. "It's broad daylight, I'm not going inside, his daughter's there, and I'm much pleasanter than Maeve. And Jane Ann will go with me. No one argues with her."

"I can go, too." Donna said.

"I don't think that's a good idea," Frannie said. "They'll think we're ganging up on them."

"I'm pretty good at asking questions, though."

Frannie thought, 'nosey, you mean?' and then felt a slight guilty twinge thinking of her own intentions but stood her ground.

"I'm just going to get my thermos and see how he is," she said.

As Larry stood, arms crossed, at the edge of the road watching, the two women headed toward Dave Schlumm's camper. The RV sat perched on its wheels and jacks, still closed up, air conditioner humming on the roof. Frannie mounted the steps and knocked. The door opened a crack and the young woman who arrived earlier peered out.

"Yes?"

"I'm Frannie Shoemaker. My husband and I sat with your dad earlier today. I think I left my thermos here."

Jodi opened the door wider. Her bleached blond hair stuck out at angles — possibly an intentional hairstyle, but more likely a result of unconsciously using it to deal with her grief.

"Come on in." Her voice was faint and raw.

"We don't want to intrude," Frannie said. "The thermos should be right there on the counter by the door."

Jodi glanced over and spotted the thermos. She reached for it and at the same time started to step out the door. Frannie backed off the steps. Jodi emerged and handed them the thermos.

"Thank you for helping Dad today," Jodi said.

"How's he doing?"

"He's sleeping." Jodi sighed. "This is really hard." Her voice caught. "I'm going to miss my mom so much. She won't get to see Aaron, my son, graduate from college or her granddaughters even start high school. It's so unfair." Tears were rolling down her cheeks now.

"I know what you mean. I lost my mom recently too, although not unexpectedly like this. I'm sure this is hard on your dad too—he will miss her a lot," Frannie said, prodding a little. "He seemed very much in shock this morning."

Jodi took a deep breath. "Yeah…he will. They hadn't gotten along very well lately, though. Dad has such a temper, sometimes I didn't know how she tolerated it."

Frannie and Jane Ann looked at each other, hiding their surprise. Dave hadn't appeared to be the one with the temper.

Frannie said, "Your dad said your mom loved this park a lot."

"She did. The only thing that really made her mad was when people abused it and didn't follow the park rules."

"Jodi, if your mom was leaving the park in her car last night for some reason and she saw something suspicious, would she have stopped and left the car or called the authorities?" Frannie asked.

"Oh, she would have tried to handle it herself. She would get so mad at people breaking rules that her emotions would get the best of her."

"Well, let us know if there's anything we can do," Jane Ann said. "We're down in sites 15 and 17. It must be extra difficult to be isolated like this, with no friends and family around."

Jodi nodded. "My brother and sister-in-law should be here tomorrow. Hopefully, the police will let us leave soon."

"Mr. Bonnard said there would be a memorial service later," Frannie said.

"Yes, she wanted to be cremated. We'll have a memorial service here in the park and scatter her ashes when all this is over." Jodi was crying again, gulping as she tried to stop. "I'm sorry—I think I need to go back in."

"Certainly." Jane Ann patted her arm. "Just let us know if we can help."

CHAPTER EIGHT

LATE SATURDAY AFTERNOON

FRANNIE AND JANE ANN walked back from the Schlumms. Frannie said, "Dave is looking more and more like the number one suspect. Funny, I certainly didn't think so this morning."

"But you know what Larry said—he may have done it in anger and now be very sorry. He has to be thinking what it will do to his kids and grandkids if it does come out that it was him."

"True."

When they returned, Donna almost attacked. "What did you find out? Anything new?"

"Dave was asleep. We just talked to his daughter outside," Frannie said.

"Maybe he's just trying to avoid you."

Frannie's shaky patience with Donna was about to fizzle out. "He's probably trying to avoid everyone. His wife just died."

The grill hung in place over the fire. Larry asked, "Is the chicken in one place or did every one bring their own?"

"It's in our fridge," Frannie answered. "I'll get it. Jane Ann's doing the sausage gravy tomorrow morning and Donna has pork chops for tomorrow night."

Mickey saluted the women and said to Larry, "We don't deserve wives who are so organized."

"Sure we do. Do I need to list all of our stellar qualities?" He followed Frannie into the camper and she handed him the plastic bag of marinating chicken breasts. After he went back out, she got out dishes, flatware and glasses. She also pulled out an inflatable ice bucket and started to blow it up for the wine. As she puffed, she looked out the back window of the camper. They had a great view of the woods from there. The late afternoon sun sifted through leaves and branches occasionally quivering with the stingy breeze. A few birds and squirrels scampered or flitted from branch to branch, testing various vantage points. Eden was at rest.

She caught a flash of color — bright yellow — and realized someone stood deep in the woods, maybe a hundred feet in. A man, small and partially hidden by the understory trees, held something yellow in one hand out in front of him. The other arm was down at his side holding the handle of a green box or suitcase. The yellow device had a familiar shape but too far away to distinguish, plus she was looking through the slats of the blinds. By the time she leaned over and parted the slats so that she could see, the man turned away from her and headed deeper into the woods. The walk, the shape, and his size made her think of Randy, Stub's friend, but she couldn't be sure.

Larry came back in the camper just then.

"Someone's out there," she said turning to him, but when she tried to point out the figure, he was gone.

"By our campsite?"

"No, in the woods. Kind of looked like that guy Randy but I couldn't be sure. He held something yellow in front of him..." She snapped her fingers. "Got it! It was a handheld GPS like ours. Looked like he also carried some kind of case. Maybe just geocaching, I guess." She breathed a sigh of relief. Geocaching was a relatively new hobby using portable GPS devices to find caches hidden by others that contained trinkets and a log that could be signed and dated if the searcher was successful. And of course a geocacher did not pose the threat that a lurking murderer would.

Larry looked puzzled. "I checked the website before we came and didn't see any caches listed for this park. Some of the state parks don't encourage it, you know."

Frannie desperately wanted a reasonable explanation that would not leave her feeling threatened. "Well, maybe another friend hid something and he has to find it. A way to pass the time."

"Could be," he agreed.

They both carried out dishes and other supper necessities. As Frannie arranged their plates and flatware on the table, she looked into the woods again behind their site. No sign of the Randy-like creature. Jane Ann noticed her staring as she set wine glasses down. "What is it?"

"When I was inside, I saw a guy out there. It looked like he had a GPS so I thought maybe he was geocaching but Larry said there aren't any caches here."

"Right," said Jane Ann. "I looked too, earlier this week." Geocaching provided an occasional diversion for both couples on their camping weekends.

"It just kind of creeped me out. Doesn't take much this weekend."

"You're having a hard time with all this. I mean, even more than the rest of us. Because of your mom?"

"Yeah, it's everything—Mother, Maeve's death, and one of the places that we've always seen as a safe haven, not so safe anymore. That's not quite right. I never thought of these parks as safe or unsafe. I never even questioned it, and now this." Frannie looked around to see who was within hearing. Rob and Donna must be getting food and dishes from their camper. "And, I have no patience with Donna. Almost everything she says gets my back up."

"As Mickey says, she is a piece of artwork," Jane Ann said, bringing a smile to Frannie's face.

"Mickey has such a way with words," she said.

"Especially for a former English teacher."

"Right. I think I could deal with Donna if we knew who killed Maeve."

Larry walked up and overheard her. "Girls, I am ordering a pleasant supper and that means no talk of murder, okay?"

"Yes, officer." Frannie smirked at Jane Ann.

"You always did think you were the boss of me," Jane Ann said to her brother. "How's that chicken coming? Looks like you're loafing on the job."

"It's about ready, and here comes the potato salad," Larry lowered his voice. "As annoying as Donna is, I've heard she makes a mean potato salad."

"Just ask her," Frannie said. Rob and Donna arrived and unloaded their contributions and everyone bustled around getting the meal on the table. Mickey threw a grubby towel over his arm and poured the wine with a flourish into the motley collection of plastic wine glasses. Larry brought over a platter of chicken and they seated themselves around the colorful table.

After a toast, Larry announced to the rest that the murder of Maeve Schlumm would be off limits in the supper conversation and they agreed, although Donna looked briefly ready to protest.

Frannie said to Mickey and Jane Ann, "Have you heard from the girls? How is their weekend going?"

Jane Ann nodded. "Mona called a little while ago and I talked to Justine too. There's a family picnic tonight with some aunts, uncles, and cousins. Their…mother…is anxious for them to meet as many of the family as possible." She paused and pushed a strand of hair back into her ponytail. "I guess it's going as well as can be expected."

"What do you hear from your kids?" Mickey asked Larry and Frannie. "Sam's changing jobs for the next school year, isn't he?" Larry had his mouth full of potato salad, so Frannie answered.

"He'll be in the same school system but is moving to a different high school. He'll be teaching more biology this year and that's his preference. He and Beth are both glad they don't have to move. The kids are so settled in their schools."

"You have a daughter too, don't you?" Donna said.

"Right. Sally is a social worker in St. Louis. She's not married but has had a steady boyfriend for about five years. No sign of wedding bells, though. Kids today.

How about you? I know about the two older boys, but don't you have a couple of girls also?" she asked Donna.

The conversation continued around children, their feats and foibles and, of course, the amazing grandchildren. At the end of the meal, they all agreed they were too full for apple cobbler and would save dessert for after the meeting. They began clearing the table and Larry nudged Frannie and nodded toward the woods. Randy walked out of the woods toward Ferraros' RV. Frannie was gratified to see that he did have a portable GPS on a strap around his neck. "He's not carrying anything else, though," Frannie said to her husband. Randy looked over and nodded when he noticed them watching him, but kept going back to his group. As they did their cleanup, Frannie tried to focus on some nebulous thought that nagged at her. When she and Larry came back out after doing their dishes, she noticed Jane Ann working on her drawings again. The fuzzy thought clicked into focus.

"Jane Ann, can I see that drawing you did of Stub's campsite again?"

Jane Ann flipped back a page and handed the sketchpad to Frannie. Larry looked over her shoulder.

"What is it?" he said.

"You're never supposed to ask an artist that question," Jane Ann said.

"I meant," Larry said, "what is bothering Frannie?"

"This," Frannie said pointing. "Remember this afternoon the sheriff or Agent Sanchez, I forget which— said they were looking for a box with slightly rounded corners? They didn't think it was a cooler because the corners on coolers are more rounded. Well, new ones are, but old metal coolers have squarer corners." She pointed at one of shapes in the drawing of the pile that Stub and his friends had pulled out of their storage compartments. "Jane Ann, do you remember this one? What color was it?"

Jane Ann sat with her chin in her hand, staring at the drawing. "Ummm, I'm pretty sure it was light green—you know, that minty color from the fifties. The color Mickey always wants to paint the bathroom. It had some writing on the side but I couldn't quite read it. After the sheriff and Agent Sanchez left, everything had been moved and I couldn't see that one anymore."

"Did it look old?" Frannie asked.

"Definitely, and the corners were not as rounded as coolers now. It was bigger than a six-pack cooler but not as big as the ones we use now. The handle is on top—kind of odd." She pointed to the top in the drawing.

"When I saw Randy in the woods earlier—and I'm sure now it was him—he was carrying something light green with a handle on top."

"What are you guys talking about?" Donna asked as she, Rob and Mickey all bent over the drawing. Frannie explained what she had seen out the window earlier. They all looked over at Stub's campsite. Randy leaned against the RV, watching them. There was no sign of an old cooler, green or otherwise.

Rob asked, "What do you think he's doing? Does it have to do with Maeve's murder?"

"I think he hid the cooler—that's why he needed the GPS. But I don't know if it has any connection to the murder or not. If he was the person I heard on the phone, he's definitely up to something fishy," Frannie said. "And, if that cooler is what was in the cave where Maeve was murdered, there has to be a connection."

"We need to stay after the meeting and talk to Agent Sanchez, let them handle it," Larry said.

"I know." Her cell rang and she looked at the screen. "Speak of the devil," she looked at Larry, "It's Sam. Hello?" She proceeded to fill their son in on events and assure him that they were fine. "I bring my own cop with me, remember? Here, I'll give you the man himself. Take care, honey. Give our love to Beth and the kids." She handed the phone to Larry. Moments later, Donna and Rob got calls and Jane Ann heard from Larry's and her mother. They must have all been watching the six o'clock news.

"Mom wondered if you had solved it yet," Jane Ann told her brother. "She still thinks you're invincible."

"I am."

"Our kids apparently don't have the same confidence. They think we're in dire danger," Rob said.

"It's about time to go to the meeting," Donna said, after hanging up with one of their daughters.

"You're so right. C'mon Cuba, this can be your evening walk," Frannie said as she unhooked the tether and hooked up the leash. Cuba gave her best 'Carry me' look but it didn't work any better than it had at any time during her 65-plus-pound adulthood. Rob put the leash on Buster and they started down the road. Stub and his friends fell in behind them.

Other campers were already walking toward the shelter near the campground entrance, kids and dogs in tow. People moved slowly and looked pretty grim, giving the appearance of heading to their own executions, but Frannie felt that impression resulted partly from the oppressive heat and humidity. Most of the campers had nothing to do with the murder and had planned on staying the whole weekend anyway. But underlying the heat was still the fact that there could be a killer among them.

When they arrived at the shelter, they found seats around a table near the back. Ranger Phillips, Sheriff Ingrham, and Agent Sanchez stood at the other end talking to a woman in the standard brown DNR uniform. Stub sat a couple of tables down with his group.

Agent Sanchez faced the group and held up his hands. The muted conversation subsided to silence as the campers all faced him expectantly.

"I have met many of you but for those I haven't, I am Warren Sanchez from the State Division of Criminal Investigation. You all know we have an unusual situation here this weekend, especially for a state park. But before we talk about that and take your questions, Ranger Phillips has some important weather information. Ranger?" Sanchez turned over the floor.

Ranger Phillips stepped forward. He was pretty comfortable in front of a group of kids with a snake or a turtle in his hands but this was new territory, and at first his voice cracked a little. He cleared his throat and started over.

"Folks, this weekend the weather is going to throw us an added curve. There's a front moving through which will bring relief from this heat but we may have a rough night ahead of us. This area is under a tornado watch until about 3:00 a.m." Some nodded, like Mickey, who had probably been glued to their weather radios, but the rest fidgeted and commented to companions in alarm. "This is Ranger Sharon Sommers, from nearby Bella Vista State Park, who has come to help us out this evening because we're short-handed." He motioned the DNR woman forward, who held up a hand in greeting. Ranger Phillips continued. "We will be monitoring the situation throughout the watch period. If we get an actual warning, we will come through the campground using a loudspeaker to ask you all to move as quickly as possible to the shower house, which is our tornado shelter. How many of you have weather radios or apps for your phones?" About twenty people, including Mickey and Larry raised their hands. "Keep those tuned and where you can hear them. Unfortunately, if anything does happen, it will most likely be middle of the night. Please keep everything you need, shoes and so forth, handy and be ready to go at a moment's notice."

Ranger Sommers then spoke up. Her voice was high and clear. "Before you go to bed, put lawn chairs and all loose items in your tents or under your RVs. Above all, take down your awnings. Not only can they be damaged, which as you know is expensive, but more importantly, in high winds they can act as a lift device, causing your RV to rock or tip." She held up one hand, palm down, demonstrating the lift of the wind. Frannie and Larry looked at each other with wry smiles, remembering just such an event several years before. They had been out in a sudden storm in the middle of the night, trying to stow their awning but too late to save it.

"It will be crowded in the shower house, if that becomes necessary," said Ranger Phillips. "We will really need everyone's cooperation. Are there any questions?"

A man near the front held up his hand. The ranger nodded at him. "If a warning comes, can't we just get in our vehicles and leave the park?"

"That's not advisable. There won't be time. The shower house is cement block and will be much safer than your car." He looked around but no one else spoke. He nodded then toward Warren Sanchez.

The agent stepped forward. "This is not what we all need, right? But it is what it is and we need to remember we are all in this together. Now, as you know, the campground host, Maeve Schlumm, died early this morning. At this time, we believe she was murdered. We have closed the park, and ask that none of you leave. Most of you planned to stay until Monday anyway. By then, we see no reason that you will be detained here any longer. We will have completed background checks by then and perhaps even know what happened. Until our investigation is complete, it is important that you stay together in groups and stay safe. We are confident that there is no threat to anyone if you do that. We have one question. Has anyone seen the people who have the Airstream in site #12 today?"

People looked at each other and shrugged or shook their heads.

"We urge you again to come to one of us if you have seen or heard anything unusual since you have been here. Are there any questions?"

Surprisingly, there were none and gradually the group dispersed with a growing din of alarmed conversation.

Larry, Frannie and Jane Ann lingered until the shelter had cleared and then walked up to the agent. Jane Ann clutched her sketchpad. Agent Sanchez watched them approach with raised eyebrows and a slightly skeptical look on his face. He's getting a little perturbed with us playing amateur Dick Tracy, Frannie realized.

"Mr. Shoemaker. Did you have a question?"

"Not exactly. But we may have some more information that could be helpful."

Agent Sanchez folded his arms. "Go on."

"This is in reference to the box you are looking for that might have been in the cave." He explained about Jane Ann's sketch and the nature of older coolers. Jane Ann showed him the sketch and pointed out the shape in question.

"Well, I wish it was a photo rather than a drawing," Sanchez said dismissively. "But we'll check it out. If it's there, it shouldn't be hard to find."

"But that's just it," Frannie said. She stuck her hands in her back pockets. "It may not be there anymore." She described seeing Randy go into the woods with the GPS and what might have been the cooler, and returning later with nothing but the GPS.

The agent scratched his head. "We'll talk to him. But it could be perfectly innocent. Doesn't seem like he would hide something illegal in broad daylight. Isn't there some game people play with a GPS—hiding things for others to find?"

Larry nodded. "Geocaching. And that could be the explanation. We just thought we should tell you."

"Sure, you're right to do that. As I said, we will check it out. Thank you." Frannie wondered at his sincerity, but they said goodbye, and walked back to the campsite.

"What do you think, Larry?" Jane Ann said when they were a short distance from the shelter. "I don't think he's taking us very seriously."

"Maybe not," Larry said. "I think he's starting to see us as the Hardy boys. But we've done all we can do."

"Maybe we could find out somehow if they still have that cooler," Frannie said.

Larry looked at her sideways. "Okay, okay. I'll be good, officer," she held up her hands in surrender.

"I'll believe that when I see it."

CHAPTER NINE

WHEN THEY GOT BACK to the campsite, River's mother sat visiting with Donna while River rolled on the ground with Buster.

His mother seemed to suddenly realize what he was doing.

"River! Get up off the ground. You'll have to take a shower!" She said it in the same tone she might say, 'You're going to have to sit in your closet for a week.' Apparently it worked, because River sat up in alarm. He jumped to his feet and brushed his clothes with amazing vigor. It was the fastest Frannie had seen anyone move all day. He then bent over to continue scratching Buster's ears.

Donna introduced them. "This is River's mom, Stephanie. Frannie and Larry Shoemaker and Mickey's wife, Jane Ann."

Frannie laughed. "He sure enjoys Buster. He said his dad was going to get him a dog like that."

Stephanie made a snorting sound. "I'd be thrilled if his dad even bought him milk and cereal."

River snapped his head up. "I'd rather have a dog than milk and cereal, Mom!"

Frannie and Donna stifled laughter while Stephanie actually guffawed. Jane Ann had gone in her camper for iced tea. "Anyone else want some? There's not a breath of air moving. Sure feels like a storm coming."

Frannie and Donna declined but Stephanie said, "I would love some. I'm worried about this storm — have you seen my little camper? A 20-mile-an-hour wind could take it."

"Do you pull the camper yourself?" Frannie asked her.

"I do now. River loves camping and when his dad left, I decided I'd better learn. My brother taught me to park it in an empty parking lot." She giggled. "It wasn't pretty but I can do it. We usually just camp here — only live about twenty miles away."

"That must be hard, raising River by yourself. Does he ever see his dad?" Jane Ann asked.

Stephanie sighed. "Not often. Trey — his dad — is usually too strung out. I never know what he'll do. He has a terrible temper. But when he's straight, he's a totally different person and that's what River remembers." She turned to Frannie. "Your husband is a cop?"

"Retired," Frannie said. "And it was small town force, so most of his job was pretty routine."

"But it makes me feel better, having him next door, in case Trey shows up."

"They have the park closed, though. No one is allowed in except the authorities."

Another sigh. "I don't think that would stop Trey. Do you mind if I sit here for a while? It's kind of lonely with just the two of us and after the murder, I couldn't let River out of my sight."

"Of course," Donna said. "Our schedule's pretty light this evening."

Stephanie smiled her thanks, acknowledging that no one in the campground had many options. Meanwhile, Cuba finally realized she was missing out on some heavy petting of the canine kind, and ambled over to River, pushing her formidable nose under the hand he was using to scratch Buster. He giggled at such persistent attention and arranged himself so he could scratch both dogs. After a few minutes, he abandoned them to come lean over the arm of his mom's chair.

"Mom? What did that policeman mean about a tornado?"

"Just that there might be one in the area tonight, and if they think so, we will all go to the shower house where we will be safe," she said.

"But what about our camper? And Buster and Cuba?" He seemed close to tears at this idea.

"Buster and Cuba will go with us," Frannie said.

"And we'll hope everybody's campers will be safe. But the important thing is that we will all be safe," Stephanie added.

Mickey held up his smart phone so River could see the screen. "It looks like the storm is going to stay south of us." River let go of his grip on his mom's arm to get a closer look at the radar image. Mickey began a detailed explanation of where they were located on the screen, what the colors meant, and which way the storm was moving.

Stephanie said. "He knows a lot about that,"

"He's a fanatic and usually drives us all nuts. But tonight it could be handy," Jane Ann said.

"River is such an unusual name," Frannie said. "How'd you come up with that?"

Stephanie gave a wry smile. "Trey wanted to call him 'Mississippi.' Can you imagine? I squelched that by telling him the nickname would end up being 'Missy.' Trey always fancied himself a modern day Tom Sawyer so we compromised on River."

"It's cool," Donna said. "It struck me as odd at first but I really like it."

The sheriff's car pulled up next to Stub's campsite and Sheriff Ingrham, Agent Sanchez and Deputy Smith got out. Stub, Randy, and their friends were in the process of putting all the coolers, boxes, and lawn chairs back in the storage compartments in preparation for the night's weather. They all straightened up as the law officers approached. Ingrham and Sanchez were there to search and gave the directive. Stub's face turned redder than it already was from exertion and he ran his hands over his thinning hair. His gestures indicated what Frannie assumed was a righteous protest over unloading the compartments for the second time that day and then loading them back up again.

"I think Stub would rather be in the worst fleabag motel around right now than in this campground," she said as the others watched the scene unfold.

"No doubt," Rob agreed.

"What's going on?" Stephanie asked.

"Looks like they're conducting a search." Larry gave Frannie a direct look that said no other information was necessary.

Jane Ann said, "Stephanie, we're going to have some apple cobbler and ice cream. Please join us; Mickey always makes enough for an army."

"Oh, that sounds great. Are you sure you have enough?"

"Believe me." Jane Ann headed to their camper.

"I'll help," Donna said.

They soon returned with a large pan of cobbler, ice cream, bowls and spoons. Mickey and River still had their heads together over Mickey's phone. "River," Mickey said. "We have a dessert warning."

River straightened up. "What's a dessert warn...?" but his eyes followed Mickey's pointing finger to the picnic table.

"Mom! Can I have some?"

Stephanie smiled and nodded. They all gathered around the fragrant pan and Donna handed out heaping bowls.

As she savored the warm cinnamony apples and crust complemented by the cool creamy ice cream, Frannie kept sneaking glances at the scene across the road. Angry grumblings from Stub's friends accompanied the officers as they efficiently pulled out, checked, and stacked the coolers and boxes around the campsite. Sanchez questioned Randy at length; then they left the stacks for the Chicago men to return to the storage compartments and went inside. Stub appeared to be questioning Randy in turn while Sanchez and Ingrham were inside, but Randy just shook his head and shrugged his shoulders, palms up.

Larry and Rob cleared the dessert things while discussing their respective golf games and Mickey and River went back to watching the radar screen.

Sanchez and Ingrham finally emerged from the motorhome empty-handed, spoke briefly to Stub, shook hands, and got in the sheriff's car. Neither man looked over at the Shoemakers and their friends, almost as if they wanted to discourage any further 'tips.' It seemed to Frannie that their earlier plea for information meant anyone but her group. She was sure Randy had hidden the old cooler in the woods, but wondered why Sanchez didn't appear to have found the GPS either. Randy must have stashed that also.

The patrol car had no sooner pulled slowly away than the two rangers appeared walking along the road, stopping here and there to reassure campers.

As they passed, Ranger Sommers asked if they needed any help tuning a weather radio. Larry shook his head and Mickey held up his smart phone.

Ranger Phillips said to Mickey, "Do you have that set to send you a message in case of a warning?"

"Yes, sir, I do."

"Good. We'll keep our fingers crossed that this passes us by but we want everyone prepared. Be sure and get as much put away as possible," he reminded them. And to Rob, "Especially those lights, if you want to keep them."

Over the last half-hour, dusk had arrived with an eerie yellow glow. The stillness and humidity seemed heavier even than it had all day. Around the campground, people packed up games, cards, books, and magazines. Lawn chairs took refuge under campers and tablecloths returned to cupboards inside. Lanterns and flashlights were placed inside within easy reach. Rob performed his lighting operations from the night before in reverse, unplugging, disassembling, coiling and storing.

Many planned to sleep in their clothes or not at all. Others scoffed and declared no storm was going to 'rob me of my beauty sleep.' Mostly false bravado. Stephanie, who had gone to secure her own campsite, returned to ask if Larry or Mickey got any early warning to please let her know. They assured her that they would make sure she and River headed to the shower house when they did.

With everything, except for a couple of chairs, as safely stowed as circumstances permitted, they perched on or sat at the picnic table as the darkness deepened. No stars twinkled above them. Mickey gave continued reports from his tiny radar screen. The storm still appeared that it would pass south of them but it also seemed to be expanding.

Stub wandered over, beer in hand.

"Are you guys crazy?" he asked, shaking his head. "You do this all the time and enjoy it? If we make it back to Chicago, we're going to forfeit what we've paid for that thing and find a nice motel somewhere."

Mickey laughed. "It really isn't usually like this. I mean, we've been through storm warnings before but I can't say that we've ever had a murder nearby before or been confined to the park." He looked at the others for confirmation as if something so trivial might just have slipped his mind.

"There have been some close calls when Jane Ann finds your stash of smokes," Larry said, straight-faced.

It was Stub's turn to laugh. "Whatever. I don't think it's the life for us. And that secret agent guy seems to think Randy is somehow involved. I mean, Randy's a grouch, and got a lot on his mind right now, but he's no murderer."

Rob said, "Well, you'll have good stories to tell for years to come."

"You guys have one of those weather radios?" Stub turned serious.

"I do," Larry said, "and Mickey has an app on his phone to get weather warnings."

"I can see where you'd need that if you did this a lot. Makes me pretty nervous. We had a tornado in the town I grew up in and you never forget that feeling—the pressure and all," Stub ran the heel of his hand across his forehead. "That was in the daytime when you could see it coming. I really don't like this middle of the night business."

Larry agreed. "This kind of weather is nothing to fool with. But the rangers and sheriff are monitoring it closely and we should be safe enough in the shower house."

Cuba ambled over and rubbed against Larry's leg.

"Looks like someone's ready for another walk," Frannie said. At the magic word, Cuba's ears sprang up, almost erect.

Larry said, "Better get it done before it starts thundering. We won't be able to peel her out of the camper."

"I guess I'd better go see what new complaints my buddies have," Stub said.

Donna and Larry hooked up walking leashes to the eager pets and Rob and Frannie joined them for a stroll around the campground. Mickey and Jane Ann volunteered to guard the campsite.

"Right!" Rob laughed. "There's nothing left that isn't tied down."

Mickey shrugged and leaned back in his lounger. "Sure, make fun. But we will be on alert protecting your butt and all you own."

"What a relief," Frannie said.

Stephanie sat at her bare picnic table with her book. River spotted them and pleaded, "Can I come with you?"

"Sure, it's just a lap to the end of the road and back," Larry said to his mother. This time, Stephanie approved. River offered to take Buster's leash from Donna and she readily surrendered it.

Progress was slow as Buster pulled River back and forth across the road investigating the wonderful smells that he found. The two couples stopped and visited a few minutes with Richard and Elaine, who introduced their fellow travelers. As they moved on, they waved or nodded at couples and families in each campsite. The scent of grilled meat still hung in the air through the campground, there being no breeze to remove it. Most of the campers had done their packing up and battening down, so people appeared at loose ends with little to do but wait for whatever the night would bring.

The asphalt road made a loop at the end of the campground bordered by tent sites. A dirt track forked off one side of the loop into the woods.

"Where does that go?" River pointed.

"To a group site back there. The Boy Scouts and other groups use it sometimes. No one's back there this weekend," Larry said.

"Can we go see?" River begged.

"Too dark," Larry said. "We didn't bring flashlights."

"Maybe tomorrow?"

"Maybe."

They continued on around the loop and back along the road to their campsite, leaving River with his mother as they passed.

Mickey sat forward in a camp chair, picking out an old folk tune on his guitar. Jane Ann perched on the camper steps, arms around her knees, humming along with the guitar. They both stopped when the walkers returned.

"Looks like you kept things safe, Mickey," Larry said. "Was it your face or your playing that did it?"

"We've had to fight off the Barbarians...to the death."

"Good man. We knew we could count on you, Mick." Frannie unhooked Cuba's leash and put her back on her tether.

Mickey had leaned his guitar against his chair and Jane Ann stood up and stretched. "I'm headed to bed. Could be a short night." She leaned over and kissed her husband, taking his guitar to store in the RV. Good nights were said and she disappeared inside.

Frannie pulled a beer out of the cooler and sat down at the picnic table. To her regret, Donna soon joined her. Larry sat by the fire ring near Mickey in the other chair and Rob set a large piece of firewood on end and perched on that. The men proceeded to solve the problems of the world — the sports world, that is.

Donna said, "Frannie, I'm sorry if I was rather abrupt yesterday about your mom. I know it's never easy."

"You weren't abrupt," Frannie lied. "I appreciate your thoughts. It's just been a hard time for me."

"Do you have any brothers or sisters?"

"No, but Larry's family has been very supportive."

"What about your dad? He's gone also?"

Frannie sighed. "He was killed in Korea when I was two."

Donna sat back. "Oh! I am sorry. Did your mother ever remarry?"

"No. I wish she had. But she felt she needed to devote all of her time to me. Then when I married and had kids, she substituted them for any other relationship. But I know she must have been lonely at times."

"Wow!" Donna said. "That is dedication."

"What about your family? You're not from around here are you?"

"No, Wisconsin. My parents have both been gone for about twenty years. And I have no siblings either."

"Now I feel bad, Donna. At least I had Mom for a long time, and she saw my kids grow up and a couple of great-grandchildren even."

In the dim light of the lantern, Donna's eyes glistened. Frannie noticed also that Donna's right hand lying on the table shook slightly. She thought about covering that hand with her own, offering comfort, something—but the moment passed. Larry stood and announced that he intended to go to bed.

103

"I'm thinking Jane Ann's got the right idea. We may be short on sleep tonight — get it while we can."

"Me too," Rob stood up and stretched.

"What is the radar showing, Mickey?" Frannie climbed out of the cramped picnic bench and arched, rubbing her lower back.

"Still moving this way but not much change. An awfully big red blob though."

"I hate those red blobs." Frannie picked up her beer can and put it in the recycling bag already stashed in the back of the pickup. Mickey and Larry put the other two chairs away. Rob and Donna took Buster and headed across the road. Frannie could see Stub and his friends still sitting next to the motorhome. Randy sat slightly out of the circle brooding while his companions tried to outdo each other with jokes and stories.

"See you in the morning," Donna called back.

"Let's hope we don't see you sooner," Mickey said.

Cuba stood up eagerly and stood by the camper steps. She knew it was cooler inside and probably sensed the imminent storm. Larry unhooked her tether and opened the door for her.

Inside, they set flashlights on the counter and Larry's flip-flops and Frannie's moccasins in the shoe caddy by the door. Frannie also took their raincoats off the hooks and laid them on the chair beside the door. Out of habit, she readied a fresh pot of coffee to plug in the next morning. Larry put the weather radio on his nightstand and made sure it was tuned in. Frannie pulled the comforter off the bed, folded it and placed it on one of the dining benches.

"Think I'll just sleep in my clothes," Larry said.

She considered a minute. "Me too. Maybe if we're fully prepared, nothing will happen." She was a great believer in unexpected things happening and expected things not.

CHAPTER TEN

SATURDAY NIGHT

FRANNIE FIRST FELT the hot smelly breath on her face and heard the rapid panting. One problem with yellow labs is that their height puts their faces right on a level with a sleeping human face. She emerged from sleep enough to hear a huge clap followed by a roll of thunder. The sound triggered a violent trembling in the dog, shaking the bed. Cuba preferred Larry's company, especially during stress and storms, but she had learned through experience that the chances of waking Frannie in the middle of the night were much better. Frannie grabbed her glasses and watch off the nightstand and pushed the glow button on the watch. 12:45. She got up, and coaxed Cuba to turn around in the narrow space.

"Back! Back!" she hissed. Cuba finally maneuvered out of the bedroom into the living area. Frannie sat on the couch, bending over to shield and reassure the dog. More claps of thunder triggered more furious shuddering. She slid off the couch to sit closer to the terrified dog. It also felt safer although she knew no reason why. Cuba was no protection in a storm. The wind began to escalate, pounding the sides of the camper. At one point, she could feel the floor underneath her actually undulate with the gusts. Rain drubbed the roof and metal sides.

Suddenly, a high shrill sound pierced the roaring of the wind. The weather radio went off at Larry's side and she heard him bolt from the bed. Nice to know something could wake him.

He pushed through the curtain at the bedroom entrance. "It's a tornado warning," he said. "Better head for the showers." He turned on the light above the sink, which would run off the battery, but noticed that the microwave indicator was not lit, so the power must be off. They slipped into shoes, put their raincoats on, and grabbed the flashlights. By the time they had Cuba on her leash and Larry got the door open, gripping the handle to keep the wind from taking it, they could hear the loudspeaker from the DNR pickup urging immediate evacuation.

Larry and Frannie rounded the end of the trailer and hit the full force of the wind and rain. Frannie bent forward, clutching her raincoat hood at her throat to keep it on her head. The rain pelted them in their faces like tiny arrows. Larry handed her Cuba's leash and motioned toward Stephanie's unit. Oral communication was out of the question. He headed to the rocking popup while Frannie continued to tug Cuba forward. Lightning and thunder cracked and crashed around her, punctuated by ominous pops from the tops of the trees. When she stopped to check on Larry's progress, someone ran into her from behind.

"Whoa!" She barely heard the exclamation but she swung her flashlight around to reveal the face of her brother-in-law. Jane Ann was clinging to his hand. Mickey mouthed "Larry?" just as the person in question appeared carrying River, covered with a blanket and Stephanie clinging to the back of his coat.

Rob and Donna caught up with them, Rob with a tight grip on a squirming Bugger. Mickey took Cuba's leash from Frannie and tugged her forward, and the rest trudged behind him. The tops of the trees waved like the fists of an angry mob demanding somebody's head. A small branch whipped across the road, catching Jane Ann on the cheek. She yelped, ducked her head, and proceeded with greater determination. As they neared the shower house, others joined them.

"Do we separate the genders?" Rob yelled when they reached the entrance.

"Just get inside," Larry growled. They started into the women's side because it was the closest but it was already jammed with people. The word went back to reverse direction and head for the men's side. Heads lowered, they hit the wind again and plodded around to the other side.

Frannie thought she too was being hit by debris on the back of her head, but then realized it was small hail. The hail provided the whole herd the needed motivation to make the last few feet to the door. About fifteen people, including Richard and Elaine and their friends, were already in the men's side when the newcomers burst in. With the power off, only emergency lights provided dim lighting. Larry set River down next to his mom, shook the wet blanket and hung it over a shower door. River clung to Stephanie's legs while Frannie grabbed some paper towels to make a pass at drying Cuba, who was still shaking violently. Jane Ann wiped her face. The paper towel came away bloody and she stood looking at it stupefied and then looked in the mirror above the sink. A long cut ran from her right cheekbone down to her mouth.

"Jane Ann, what happened?" Frannie asked, alarmed.

"I got hit with something back there—I think it's just superficial" She ripped off another paper towel and held it to her cheek.

The door opened again, letting in the roar of the wind. Stub and several of his buddies hurried in followed by a couple of families. Stub's face lit up when he saw the Shoemakers and their friends, as if he had completed a pilgrimage across an ocean instead of a few hundred feet down the road. The wind started creating odd noises in the roof and they looked up in alarm. Mickey studied the screen of his phone.

"There's a 'hook' here in this mass and that often means a tornado, but it's still south of us and moving straight east right now. We might squeak by," he said.

"Let's hope so," Larry said, still eyeing the ceiling.

"Lar, this is somethin', huh?" Stub said, shedding his poncho. He spoke with bravado, trying to cover his nervousness. The room was getting crowded now. Stub introduced the two men behind him but the increasing roar of the wind drowned out his voice and Larry just nodded. Others gave up trying to talk over the noise and huddled with their companions. Frannie and Larry slid to the floor against the wall. Frannie wanted to close her eyes or hide her face on Larry's sleeve but was afraid to miss what was happening. They sat looking up at the roof, Cuba wedged in between them. As quickly as it had built, the noise subsided.

Frannie said to Larry, "Was that actually a tornado, do you think?"

He shrugged but Stub heard her and shook his head. "Maybe close by but not here."

Just then the strains of "Amazing Grace" wafted over the wall from the women's side.

"They're singing!" someone said.

"At least it's not 'Nearer My God to Thee,'" Frannie said. Everyone quieted for a moment to hear old hymn punctuated by intermittent crashes of thunder.

The door opened again, breaking the spell, and Ranger Phillips entered. He nodded to several of them and pulled a clipboard out from under his poncho. He began working his way through the crowd, checking off names and asking questions as he went. When he got to Stub, Stub looked around for his companions. He could only find three.

"Who's missing?" Ranger Phillips asked.

"Uh, Randy...and Darryl."

"Were they with you when you headed here?"

"Yeah! We all left the motorhome at the same time."

"Ranger Sommers is checking the women's side. Maybe they went over there."

Stub nodded, but didn't look convinced.

Phillips finished checking off everyone in the men's side and left to compare notes with Sommers.

"I think the wind is dying down a little bit," Larry said. He and Frannie got to their feet—cement floors quickly became uncomfortable.

"Do you think we had a tornado?" Stephanie asked him.

"I don't think so, but we could have some wind damage."

Stephanie looked glum.

Frannie patted her on the back. "Keep your fingers crossed. The important thing is that we are all okay."

Stephanie gave a weak smile and nodded. Several people sat on the floor using the wall as a back support. Stephanie and Frannie had to be careful not to step on someone. River tugged on his mom's sleeve.

"What's happening, Mom? Are we gonna be okay?"

She roughed up his spiky hair even more. "We're fine. I think the storm's almost over."

"Good!"

Donna sitting on the floor, pulled a pack of cards out of her raincoat pocket.

"River! Do you know how to play Slap Jack?"

He looked skeptical. "Nope."

"It's easy. We divide up the cards and lay them down one at a time face up like this." She demonstrated. "If one of us lays down a jack," she held one up for him to see, "whoever slaps the pile first gets the whole pile! The one with the most cards at the end wins."

River, like most kids, was intrigued by the physical aspects. "Show me that jack again."

112

Donna handed him a card to look at. "See that 'J' up in the corner? Do you know the letter 'J'?"

River nodded seriously. "My *other* name is John. I can spell it."

"Your other...oh, you mean, your middle name?"

"Yeah, River John Ballard."

"Well, sit down and let's play."

He collapsed to the floor next to Bugger in one fluid motion that was the envy of everyone in the room over thirty, ending cross-legged. Donna expertly dealt the cards. River checked each one before he laid it down, so he was well prepared to slap at the appropriate times—and a few times it wasn't. Soon several other kids gathered around and were taken into the game. The adults stood around smiling at the delight created by a simple, silly game. Frannie remembered Donna stating earlier that she didn't play games. Amazing how a child could overcome adult quirks.

The door opened again and Ranger Phillips hurried in. The sound of the storm when the door was open had definitely decreased.

"Folks, the warning has been lifted, so you are free to return to your camping units. I think we dodged the bullet this time. There are some limbs down and a few tents blown over, but no serious damage as near as we can tell. We'll see what daylight brings, but Sharon and I will be around tonight to help you with tent problems."

Those who were sitting stood and gathered belongings. People began to file out the door. The ranger motioned for Stub to wait.

"Your friend Darryl is next door but no sign of Randy Burton. I've notified Agent Sanchez since Mr. Burton is currently a person of interest, but we want you to check and make sure he didn't stay in the motorhome."

Stub almost looked sick. He nodded to the ranger and pulled his poncho over his head.

"Let's get out of here," Larry said to Frannie. He picked River up again since the boy had no shoes on. Stephanie and Frannie leading Cuba followed him out the door. The Nowaks and the Ferraros had gone ahead. On the sidewalk leading from the shower house, Larry stopped and looked back, then up at the peak of the shower building. "Siding blew off from up there," he said. "That's the noise I heard when I thought it might be taking the roof."

The rain had stopped and a fresh breeze blew from the north.

"Look, River," Larry pointed at the glimpse of sky through the trees. "Stars! The storm is definitely over." River looked up and back at Larry with a wide grin. He gave Larry a tight hug and his relief was almost palpable. Cuba trotted along sensing the atmospheric change that confirmed the end of the storm. As they returned to their campsites, they could see a few limbs askew in the tops of the trees silhouetted against the sky.

"Look, Mom!" River shouted, causing Larry to wince. "Our camper's okay!"

Stephanie smiled up at him. "You bet, honey." She held up her arms. "I can take him from here, Larry. Thanks for all your help."

Larry surrendered River and glanced around Stephanie's campsite. Satisfied that nothing appeared damaged, he took Frannie's hand and they both waved goodnight to River and his mom.

"That bed's going to feel good. Even better since the temperature has dropped quite a bit. I think we can turn the air off and open the windows," Larry said. The rest of the group waited for them at their campsite.

"Well, Camp Director, what fun surprises do you have planned for us tomorrow?" Rob grinned at Larry.

"I think we have boredom on the schedule," Larry replied, slapping Rob lightly on the back of the head. "And, complaints will not be tolerated."

Stub was coming toward them, a disturbed expression on his face—almost fear, Frannie thought.

"Larry, Randy isn't here. We can't find him." Stub pulled a handkerchief out of his pocket and mopped his forehead, even though it was the coolest it had been all day.

Larry sighed. Frannie knew he was tired, and tired of being expected to solve everyone's problems, even though he never complained about it. Just like people expected teachers to also teach Sunday School, lead Cub Scouts, chaperone 4-H trips, and everything involving leading kids, they expected even off-duty policemen to find answers.

"Stub, you have to let Agent Sanchez and the sheriff handle this. I have no official standing and they don't like me interfering."

"I know, but they think Randy is a murderer. I've known him for years, Larry. He didn't do this."

"Could he have been injured in the storm and wandered off?" Mickey asked.

"I don't know. I don't know what to think." Stub plopped down on the bench of their picnic table and quickly jumped back up again when the damp left from the storm seeped through the seat of his pants. Frannie snuck a look at Larry. He had that 'Now we'll never get to bed' look on his face.

But he said, "Stub, I think you're going to have to talk to the agent. Here he comes."

"Mr. Berger," Sanchez said. He was a lot less dapper looking at 2:30 in the morning than he had been the day before.

"Yes, sir," Stub answered.

"Where's your friend Randy?"

"I don't know, sir. I'm afraid something has happened to him."

"I think it's more likely that he saw a chance to get out of here."

Stub shook his head. "I don't think so. I don't think Randy has had anything to do with what's been going on around here this weekend."

"You're his friend."

"Of course, and I know he would never hurt anyone else."

"My point is, you're hardly objective. We have put out an APB for him. We'll also search around here in case something *did* happen to him on the way to the shower house, but I doubt it. There wasn't that much damage."

Stub's shoulders slumped and he looked thoroughly beaten. "I'll help search," he said.

"Suit yourself," Sanchez replied. "We'll just go along the road tonight; a more thorough search will have to wait for daylight."

"We can help too," Mickey said, indicating his friends with a nod of his head.

The agent nodded. "Bring flashlights."

Frannie grabbed Jane Ann's arm and said, "We'll catch up with you. First I'm going to play nurse on Jane Ann's face."

117

Jane Ann protested but Frannie hauled her into her camper in pursuit of the first aid kit. Jane Ann took the tube of ointment out of Frannie's hand and headed for the bathroom mirror.

"I will take care of it myself!" she said.

"I wasn't even going to use iodine," Frannie called after her. Soon she was back, and, with flashlights, they followed the rest of the group.

They had split up and were walking along both sides of the road, shining their lights along the road and behind trees, calling Randy's name. Frannie couldn't help but think of the scene in the musical *Brigadoon* where the villager men give chase and sing "Harry Beaton! Harry Beaton!" before Mr. Beaton could escape and doom the village to sleep forever.

Could Randy Burton bring the same fate? She allowed herself a little smile, thinking sleeping forever sounded pretty good right now. They continued on past the shower house to the end of the campground on the chance that Randy could have become disoriented in the storm. They circled each campsite, checking behind tents and campers. Flashlight beams bounced and lanterns glowed at two sites where the rangers helped struggling campers right and secure their tents. Agent Sanchez stopped to ask them about the missing man and received only shaking heads in response.

When they reached the end of the campground, Sanchez stopped and said, "We can't do any more until morning. Would he have a cell phone with him?"

"I don't know," Stub said. "We left the motorhome in such a hurry. But he usually carried it."

"Have you got his number?"

"In my phone," Stub pulled it out of his pocket.

"Call it," the agent directed.

Stub punched several buttons and held the phone to his ear. Nothing for a minute and then said "Hello? Randy? Oh…no… thanks. No, nothing yet."

He snapped the phone shut. "That was Darryl. Randy's phone was laying on the counter in the motorhome."

"So much for that," Sanchez said. "Before I go, Mr. Berger, I would like that cell phone." Stub nodded miserably. "Let's all get some sleep. We can't do anything more tonight. We'll start a search at daybreak. Any of you want to volunteer to help, I'd appreciate it."

They all murmured something noncommittal and headed back to their respective units.

When they got back in their trailer, Frannie said, "I agree with Agent Sanchez. Seems most likely that Randy took the opportunity to escape."

"Well, like we said earlier, Randy could be involved in something totally unrelated to Maeve's murder, but could get him in a lot of trouble anyway. I'm still liking Dave Schlumm for the murder. Did you see him and his daughter in the shower house?"

"As we were leaving, I did. They had been in the women's side." She laid her glasses and watch on the nightstand. As she did, she noticed a piece of paper that looked like it has been torn from a yellow legal pad.

She held it up to show Larry. "Leave it alone," she read.

"What?"

Her eyes were wide and her heart pounded a little faster. She held out the slip of paper.

"This note. It was on my nightstand. It says 'Leave it alone.' I don't know where it came from. It wasn't there when we went to bed the first time tonight."

Larry bolted up in bed to peer at the paper in her hand. "Someone put it there when we were helping search for Randy? They came all the way in and left it by the bed?"

Frannie nodded. "Or while we were in the shower house. We didn't lock the camper either time."

"But everyone else was in the shower house too."

"Except Randy."

He took the note from her. It was printed in block letters with a pencil.

"It seems more like a warning than a threat," she said. "You know what I mean?"

"No, I *don't* know what you mean." He considered it a threat and an invasion of their home-away-from-home and he didn't like her trying to make light of it.

"Well, there's no punctuation, no emphasis, no underlining, no 'or else!!!'"

He shook his head. "You're crazy. This is not a movie or a game. The fact that there is a note and left where it was is enough to make it a threat."

She crawled into bed and lay thinking about what he said. Someone was in here without their permission or knowledge, another violation of their peaceful place. What was going on? What were they supposed to leave alone? Maeve's murder? She thought about their suspicions — especially of Dave and Randy. But they were only suspicions and punctuated by huge gaps in the puzzle.

In spite of her exhaustion, she could not sleep. It was quiet and cooler — perfect sleeping weather. But she lay and stared at the reflection on the ceiling from the night light out in the living area. Every so often, she picked up her watch and looked at it. 3:10. 3:45. The last time she looked at it, it read 4:05 before she slipped into oblivion.

CHAPTER ELEVEN
EARLY SUNDAY MORNING

IN SPITE OF HER late night, Frannie woke about 6:00 and lay looking at the soft morning light coming through the window blinds on her side of the bed. Suddenly she remembered the early morning search Agent Sanchez had planned. She sat up. Larry was already gone. She got up and, welcoming the early morning chill, pulled on old gray sweat pants and a hooded sweatshirt and brushed her teeth. Outside, Cuba lay already tethered and raised her head to check out Frannie with only mild interest. She dropped her head back on the ground, worn out from too much excitement and activity the night before. There was no human activity that Frannie could see, and certainly none that Cuba was interested in.

The morning air was crisp and twenty degrees cooler than the morning before. At first it seemed like typical early morning quiet, but as Frannie listened, she could make out the distant sounds of people going through the woods. She headed straight out from the campsite into the woods in the direction Randy had gone the afternoon before.

Stepping over branches and watching out for poison ivy and stinging nettle, she fervently wished that a steamy mug of coffee would appear on one of the stumps along the way. She hadn't even thought to bring water. However, there was plenty on the ground. About every third step, her foot sunk into mud or a small pool of rainwater. At first she headed downhill into a gully, and as she got close to the bottom, she caught a glimpse of a couple of people going up the other side. They were moving slowly back and forth using walking sticks to check the underbrush. She could hear occasional calls of "Randy! Randy Burton!" Brigadoon again.

Bug spray. She had forgotten that also and spent a lot of energy swatting the pests. She could see now that one of the searchers directly ahead of her was Mickey.

"Mickey! Wait up!"

He turned and waved. She huffed and stumbled up the hill until she caught up with him.

"Good morning, Sleeping Beauty." He gave her one of his famous — or infamous — grins.

"Couldn't get to sleep last night, as tired as I was. Why is it always like that?" She batted the mosquitos swarming around her head.

"Bug juice?" he asked producing a bottle from a cargo pocket.

"You are a lifesaver!" She took the bottle from him and splashed some on her face, neck and arms, smelling like a chemical lab.

"I guess that's what we're all trying to do." He became serious, unusual for him.

"Is everyone searching this direction or did they split up?"

"Our group is all out here with Smith and Phillips. Stub and his friends went the other way from the campground with Sanchez and the sheriff. Larry should be over to our right somewhere."

"Well, I'll move over that way." She went about forty feet from Mickey and they continued their search. As they moved forward, she occasionally caught a glimpse of Larry through the trees, farther to her right. Nearing the top of the hill, they had to climb over or skirt more and more fallen limbs and trees.

"Is this damage all from last night?" she called over to Mickey.

"Looks pretty fresh."

At the top of the hill they came out in a small clearing. Donna and Rob were already there along with Ranger Phillips off to Mickey and Frannie's left, picking burrs off the bottoms of their sweat pants. Larry, Jane Ann, and Deputy Smith emerged from the trees to the right. Everyone's shoes were caked with mud and their arms, if uncovered, peppered with scratches and bites.

"Hey, Lazy Bones!" Larry said when he saw his wife.

"I know. Embarrassing." She was almost always the first one up.

Larry addressed the group. "I take it no one has seen anything?" They all shook their heads. "Frannie, did you bring your phone?"

She shook her head. No coffee, no water, no bug repellent, no phone. As a searcher, she was a failure.

"Stay near Mickey then."

Deputy Smith said, "I think we'll just continue on the other side of the clearing. I'll check in with the sheriff first and see if they've had any luck." She pulled out her radio. After a very short conversation, she keyed off the radio and said to the others, "Nothing. Let's keep going."

Frannie trudged along behind Mickey and when they got to the trees, they split up again. She took special care to look under piles of brush and fallen trees, whether they appeared recent or not. She was checking one of those when she came around a fairly tall witch hazel and saw a familiar bit of yellow. A black strap was caught on a branch and underneath hung a portable GPS. Like she and Larry had. Like Randy had the day before. She didn't touch it but called for Mickey and Larry instead.

While she waited, she looked carefully around the area. Ahead and slightly right, there seemed to be more broken branches than usual. Mickey was closer and got there first.

"Whoa!" he said. "Isn't that what Randy was carrying yesterday when you saw him?"

She nodded. Although what it meant hanging on the tree, she had no idea. Larry crashed through the brush and came to a halt as she pointed. Frannie thought their surprise was because none of them, including her, had really expected to find anything—that Randy was long gone. Larry pulled out his phone and called Sanchez.

"What did he say?" Frannie asked when Larry got off the phone after describing the find and where they were.

"He's coming and bringing the rest with him. We'll search more intensively from here."

Jane Ann caught up with him and she too was speechless at the sight of small GPS device.

Deputy Smith followed her. "Have you already notified the others?"

Larry nodded.

Frannie said, "Larry, it might be helpful to check the waypoints. I'm sure that GPS has something to do with all this. Randy had it yesterday when he was out here on his mysterious errand and now it shows up again. Maybe one of the waypoints would tell us where he went. Or else why would he even have had it with him?"

"We can't touch it until Sanchez gets here. We'll have him check." Larry called Rob and told his group also to wait up until the agent arrived.

The five of them waiting presented a stationary target for the bugs. Mickey got out his bug spray and passed it around. Rob and his group walked over from their left.

Rob eyed the suspended electronic device. "Does that work like one in a car?"

"Basically," Larry said. "Ours is pretty simple. You can mark where you are and find your way back to that spot or enter coordinates from another source to find something."

Frannie added, "You can download current maps so that you can use it for navigation like the ones you're talking about. We don't do that because we just use it for geocaching."

When Sanchez and the other searchers arrived, Larry pointed out the location of the device. Sanchez held everyone else back and moved closer. He pulled a pen from his shirt pocket and used it to unhook the strap from the branch.

Holding it aloft, he cocked his head at Larry. "You know how to see what he has programmed in this?"

"Sure, we have one just like it."

"What about a password?"

"They usually don't use one."

Sanchez pulled a pair of disposable gloves from a pants pocket. "Here put these on."

Larry slipped the gloves on easily and turned the GPS on. While waiting for it to locate the satellites, he noticed that it was the high sensitivity model, which meant it would do better in the trees. He paged to the Waypoints screen and pushed 'enter.' Frannie peered over his shoulder as they examined the alphabetical and numerical choices. He looked at her.

"Start with '1', I guess?" she said and shrugged.

He did and when he got the description, shook his head. "That one's 220 miles east of here." He tried number 2 with no better results.

"Maybe it's under 'B' for Bat Cave," Frannie said.

The A-D category produced no nearby results.

"Wait!" Frannie knocked herself in the head with the heel of her hand. "Go back to the Waypoints list. Isn't there a 'closest' or something choice at the bottom?"

He did as instructed and smiled at her. "'Nearest.' Good thinking. Let's hope he only used this once while he's been here." He selected 'nearest' and a screen popped up listing several waypoints by proximity.

"Number 13 is only 430 feet," he straightened up and took a couple of steps and pointed in the general direction they had been going. "That way."

Agent Sanchez almost smiled. "All right. Let's fan out again, but not too far, and head that direction. Larry will lead. Step carefully, although I imagine the storm probably washed out any evidence."

Stub said, "Wait a minute. If he lost the GPS, how was he going to head in that direction?"

Frannie responded before Sanchez could. "We think he used the GPS to hide something earlier…"

Sanchez finished for her. "It's the only clue we have. Maybe he headed back there." No one mentioned that he might have just run away.

They started moving forward again, Larry slightly ahead. The brush seemed thicker here and broken in many places. Frannie tripped on a root but caught herself on a tree trunk before she went down completely. The going got even slower. They hadn't gone a hundred feet before they heard Rob yell, "Over here!" A note of panic quavered in his voice.

Larry came up behind Frannie and took her hand as they worked their way toward Rob. He stood looking at the ground with Donna hanging on his arm. Ranger Phillips stood aside talking into his radio. Frannie could see others weaving through the trees back to Rob. None of the searchers had had time to get very far away.

Rob stared down at the body of Randy Burton crumpled facedown partially under a thicket of serviceberry. Deputy Smith was right behind Larry and Frannie, and again instructing everyone else to stay clear of the area, she crouched down next to the body, checking for signs of life. She shook her head and stood up. Agent Sanchez arrived with Stub right behind him.

Frannie watched Stub's face as he saw and comprehended the loss of his friend. She moved around beside him. "Stub. Maybe you should sit down over here on this log." She took his arm gently and motioned toward a fallen tree about ten feet away.

He allowed himself to be led, but said weakly "Is he — ?"

"I think so," Frannie said in a soft voice. "Agent Sanchez will tell us what we can do." She sat down on the log herself and pulled him down beside her. He covered his face with his hands, elbows supported on his knees. He started to shake and she realized he was crying.

"How did this happen?" He choked. "It was just a bunch of guys, trying to have a good time, a little vacation. But it was doomed from the beginning. It's my fault…I set the whole thing up."

"Stub, listen to me." She tried to peer into his face and patted his knee. "It's not your fault. We don't know who did this or why, but it wasn't your doing."

Agent Sanchez called for everyone's attention. "Thank you all for your help this morning. I would like you all to return to your campsites and wait there. Ranger Phillips will go with you. The crime scene crew and the medical examiner are on their way and the ranger can guide them out here." He turned back to the body without waiting to make sure they followed his instructions. They headed back to the campground in twos and threes, Stub between Larry and Frannie. His friends walked ahead and didn't seem very concerned with Stub's distress.

When they reached the campsite, Frannie said to Stub, "I'm going to put some coffee on. Didn't have time earlier. Would you like some?"

"I'd better get back to my group..." Stub looked across the road where his four remaining buddies were deep in conversation and ignoring him. "Sure, that sounds good. I really appreciate all the help you and Larry have given me. Those guys really didn't know Randy."

"This has got to be so hard, I can't even imagine. Take a seat, Stub. I have the pot all ready to go. It will just take a few minutes." She climbed the steps into the camper, grabbed the old percolator off the counter where she had prepared it the night before, and brought it out and plugged it in. Larry sat across the picnic table from Stub. Stub looked thoroughly beaten. What a change, Frannie thought, from the brash, over-confident man who had arrived Friday night.

"We generally just go on weekend trips," Larry was saying. "We like the state parks in eastern Iowa and western Illinois but there are a lot of nice county parks and several great Corps of Engineers facilities around here, too."

Stub nodded and sighed. "I'm sure it's fun when you know what you're doing." He didn't sound convinced. "You were a cop. Do you think Randy was hit by something in the storm last night—something natural, I mean — or is this another murder? Wouldn't two murders in the same park in two days be an awful coincidence?"

Larry nodded. "Yes it would, unless they're connected. But we won't know until Sanchez completes his investigation."

Frannie joined them at the table. The other two couples were giving them some space, Rob and Donna at their trailer and Mickey and Jane Ann building a fire. "Did Randy have a family?"

"He has one son in college. He and his wife have been divorced for five or six years." Stub looked, if possible, even more miserable at the thought of notifying the family.

"Oddly enough," he said, "This trip was actually Randy's suggestion, even though he blamed me when stuff started to go wrong. And he's the one yesterday who wanted to keep going after all that had happened."

Frannie thought about that while Larry changed the subject to Stub's family. Why would someone who was so not having a good time want to continue? She remembered the delivery mentioned in the mysterious phone call the day before. If it was Randy on the phone — and she was becoming more and more convinced that it was — could that be his motive for continuing this trip that was so obviously making him miserable? And what did it all have to do with Maeve? She realized then that with the discovery of Randy's body, they had stopped short of finding the location of waypoint 13.

The coffee finished and she filled three mugs. "Do you take cream or sugar?" she asked Stub, setting the mug in front of him. He shook his head so she placed the container of sweetener and a spoon in front of Larry.

She had just settled back at the table and looked up to see Stub's remaining traveling companions head back across the road toward them. Apparently, they had thought better of their behavior because the one called Darryl said, "You okay, Stub?" All he got was a noncommittal shrug. "Hey, look, we know this wasn't your fault..." Darryl jealously eyed Stub's coffee.

"Would you all like some coffee?" Frannie asked, starting to get up.

"That would be great," Darryl said. "We didn't bring a coffee pot." Stub winced, another black mark against him.

Larry grabbed Frannie's wrist. "Sit," he ordered. "I'll get the mugs." Rob and Donna were returning, too. Mickey walked over and said, "I'll put our pot on. I think we're going to need it."

By the time everyone who wanted it had coffee and found seats around the fire, Agent Sanchez appeared at the edge of the campsite. They all looked up expectantly.

"Was it storm-related?" Rob asked.

"Not likely," Sanchez said. "He was strangled."

The news fell like a rock. The Shoemakers' group grew serious, even alarmed, but Randy's traveling companions looked positively stricken.

Stub swallowed and looked at the agent. "Where will they take him?"

"They'll have to take him to the county hospital for the autopsy."

Without a word, Stub set his mug down, got up, trudged over to the motorhome, and went in.

Larry offered coffee to Agent Sanchez, who accepted. "You didn't follow the GPS to the coordinates for that waypoint, did you?" he asked the agent.

"Not yet. I'd like to have you help me do that. But I would like to turn Randy's over to the technicians. You said you have one just like it?"

"Sure. Let's go inside and we'll get the coordinates off Randy's. We have something else to show you." Frannie followed them into the camper. She went back to the bedroom to get the note. Sanchez sat down at the dinette and pulled out a plastic bag with the GPS in it. He put on disposable gloves and removed the device from its bag. Larry got out their GPS and showed Sanchez on it how to navigate to the waypoints and the coordinates. Sanchez read off the coordinates for waypoint 13 and Larry entered them in his own device.

"Check the next nearest waypoint also." Larry showed him how to do that. One other point entered in the GPS appeared to be in the vicinity of the park so Larry copied those down too.

Frannie stood watching them and when Sanchez finished, she laid the note on the table in front of him. "This was on my nightstand last night when we came in after the tornado warning and the search."

Sanchez examined it and looked up at both of them. "I think you have been meddling too much. I shouldn't have to tell you—," directing this to Larry, "—that this is serious business."

"We have been trying not to meddle," Larry said, speaking mostly for himself.

"Maybe so, but what is obvious now is that whatever Randy was up to, he's not the only one. The danger is not gone. Do you think this note is from him?"

"He was the only one not in the shower house during the warning, but it could have been left here when we were helping you search for Randy after the warning," Frannie said. "I'm becoming convinced that the phone call I overheard yesterday was Randy. Did you check his phone for outgoing calls yesterday afternoon?"

"Yes, ma'am," Sanchez said with a smirk. "Before you wrap up this investigation, you should probably know there were three outgoing calls to the same number."

Frannie ignored his sarcasm "Well, maybe that's it! Do you know whose number it is?"

"As a matter of fact, we do. It belongs to the local funeral home. According to the assistant mortician, who took the call, Mr. Burton arranged to have flowers sent to Maeve Schlumm's family. Apparently he felt pretty bad about mouthing off to her the night before."

"Oh." Frannie plopped down on the other side of the dinette, discouraged. "Well, maybe it wasn't Randy I heard. The person on that call certainly wasn't ordering flowers."

Sanchez stood. "I'll take this GPS down to the techs and then when I come back we'll use yours to see where those coordinates are." They followed Sanchez out the door and rejoined their group. The Chicago crew had returned across the road.

Mickey said, "Not to make light of it, but this finding a body every morning is getting old in a hurry."

Jane Ann looked at her watch. "It's only 9:00. Do you still want to do the sausage gravy and potatoes this morning?"

Frannie said, "Agent Sanchez will be back and wants us to go with him to find the coordinates on Randy's GPS. The rest of you can go ahead, though."

"Why don't we wait until tomorrow morning for the gravy and just do our own thing today. Will that work?" Donna asked, looking at Jane Ann.

"No problem."

Frannie and Larry filled water bottles, took a couple of granola bars, and made sure they had a bottle of repellent. They sat down to wait for the agent's return.

Donna said, "We need to take Buster for a walk. Can we take Cuba, too?"

"That would be great." Frannie looked at the old dog whose ears perked up at the sound of her name and the magic word in the same paragraph. "Poor girl, we totally forgot about you in the ruckus this morning, didn't we?" She leaned over and administered an ear scratch.

"This certainly shoots down Randy as a suspect in Maeve's murder, doesn't it?" Mickey said.

"Well, if it was him, it means he wasn't working alone," Larry replied. He looked at his wife, who had gotten up to get Cuba's leash. "Is that my sweatshirt?"

Frannie looked down at what she was wearing. She straightened her arms and the sleeves covered her hands. She grinned. "Maybe."

"Are you out of clothes, Frannie? Do we need to go shopping?" Jane Ann said.

"Excellent idea, Jane Ann, but I don't think the sheriff would consider it a necessary reason to leave the park."

"Oh yeah. That."

THE DNR PICKUP pulled up and parked. Ranger Phillips and Sanchez got out and walked over. Phillips looked especially shaken and fretful.

"Ready?" Sanchez asked. Frannie and Larry gathered up their supplies and Larry powered on the GPS. The four headed out single file along the same route they had taken earlier that morning. The foliage had dried some so the going was a little easier. Halfway down into the first ravine, Frannie broke the silence.

"Have they taken Randy—?"

"They're doing that now," Sanchez answered. "They'll take him out a shorter route." They plodded on, reaching the still muddy bottom. They climbed the other side and walked through the small clearing. Entering the woods on the other side, they soon came to the spot where Frannie had found the GPS. Through the trees off to the left, the medical examiner, the sheriff and Deputy Smith could be barely seen supervising the removal of Randy Burton's body.

Larry checked the GPS and pointed ahead and off to the right. "We need to go that way."

"We're not too far from the edge of the park," Ranger Phillips said.

"Interesting," Sanchez said.

"How far to the waypoint?" Frannie asked Larry.

"357 feet."

They all stared in the direction Larry had pointed as if some kind of X-ray vision would reveal the target that seemed to have cost Randy his life. Larry once again led the way.

Frannie stopped to take swig of water and glanced around as she snapped the lid back on. The trees looked freshly washed and the crisp air sharpened every leaf and twig. The beauty was almost painful considering the circumstances. She hurried to catch up with the others. Larry occasionally called back the distances. "250 feet — 175 feet — 100 feet — 50 feet." When he got to 20 feet, he stopped and pointed at a clump of multiflora rose ahead.

"Looks like it's going to be in that mess."

"How accurate is that thing?" Sanchez asked.

"Usually within a couple of feet."

They circled around the multiflora rose, considered a noxious weed in Iowa and several other states and not to be confused with the state flower, the wild prairie rose. The ten-foot high branches climbed a nearby soft maple and arched back to the ground, taking root again and forming a tangle as formidable as any barbed wire. Brayton Phillips used a long stick to lift masses of branches so they could peer underneath. If something had been hidden there, it wasn't there now. But evidence of the leaves and dirt being disturbed caused Phillips to shine his flashlight on the area.

Sanchez crouched, hands on knees, staring at the spot. "I believe," he said, "the same container that was in the cave has been here." He took the flashlight from Phillips and focused it on the area nearest the tree trunk. "See the rounded corners?"

"How far is the edge of the park from here?" Frannie asked Phillips.

"If you look through those trees, you can just see a bit of fence. That's an old dirt road on the other side of the fence."

"Maybe that's how the murderer has been entering the park."

Sanchez shook his head. "Maybe, but the conundrum in this case is motive. If the killer isn't in the campground, is he—or she—trying to deliver or pick something up? Stub doesn't remember there ever being an old green cooler, such as your friend described, loaded in that motorhome. Why would someone bring it in and then take it away again?"

Frannie had an idea about that but didn't think Sanchez would give it much credence. He proceeded to wrap the multiflora thicket with yellow crime scene tape. "Well, let's head back." He nodded to the ranger to take the lead.

CHAPTER TWELVE

LATE SUNDAY MORNING

WHEN THEY ARRIVED BACK at the campsite, Mickey and the Nowaks were enjoying a light breakfast at the picnic table, joined by Stephanie and River. Donna had changed from her early morning sweats into a red t-shirt with a large sequined 'USA' on the front in blue and white and jeans. Frannie thought maybe she was trying to compete with her husband's lights. Jane Ann sat in one of the loungers, an ice pack on her knee. The scrape on her cheek from the branch the night before looked pretty angry. In spite of that, she looked her usual crisp self in a pale green shirt and dark green shorts.

"Jane Ann! What happened?" Frannie asked.

"Oh, just stupid. I must have twisted my knee out in the woods. It doesn't take much. After you guys went back out, I noticed it was starting to swell."

Frannie poured out her cold coffee and refilled it from Mickey and Jane Ann's pot. "Sounds like one of my tricks. You're usually more graceful than that. You look like you've been hit by a truck. Better take it easy today… no cooking, no picking up, no waiting on Mickey…" she said.

"Now wait a minute," Mickey objected. "That's what she's here for!"

"Neener, neener," said his wife.

Donna said, "I think she should go to the emergency room. I'd be glad to take her. They'd have to let us out for that!" It disgusted Frannie that Donna was so transparent in her motive for being helpful.

"I'm fine," Jane Ann said. "I'll just stay off it the rest of the day." And then looking at Mickey, "or year."

"What happened to that agent?" Stephanie asked.

"He and the ranger cut back to the ranger residence," Larry said, following Frannie to the pot.

Frannie noticed the worried expression on Stephanie's face. "Is something wrong?"

"Trey—my husband—was here this morning, early. He said he just wanted to make sure we were okay after the storm, but the agent said I had to be sure and report it if he showed up."

Larry frowned. "How did he get into the park?"

"Oh, he's hunted around here for years—not in the park...I don't think—but he knows every road in the area. He came in some back way."

"Did he threaten you?"

"No, he was sober and he's never mean then." Stephanie looked a little surprised. "I think he actually was worried about us. We didn't even know about that other guy getting killed then."

Frannie believed that Stephanie didn't know but she wasn't so sure about the wayward husband. If Randy was involved in a drug drop, Trey could have been a likely accomplice. But she couldn't imagine how they would have made contact with Randy being from Chicago. On the other hand, she wasn't exactly an expert on how the drug trade operated.

Larry asked, "Do you want me to let Agent Sanchez know of his visit?"

"I would appreciate it," Stephanie said. She probably had enough of dealing with the authorities about Trey.

"What time was he here?"

"You were all gone, searching. I was scared at first until I could see that he was okay. I think it was about 8:00."

"I'll walk down and tell him," Larry said.

After he left, Frannie peeled an orange and fixed herself some toast. She had just gotten comfortable in her camp chair when Jodi Schlumm and her father walked up. She started to get up to greet them but Jodi motioned her back in her seat.

"I'm sorry. We're interrupting. Dad and I just wanted to thank you for all your help yesterday."

Dave Schlumm looked more collected than the day before. Hair combed, shirt clean and eyes clearer. He offered his hand to Frannie, looking around. "Is your husband here? 'Fraid I wasn't more than a lump yesterday."

"That's very understandable. He'll be back soon. He just walked down the road."

Donna said to Jodi, "We saw you drive by a while ago. Did they let you leave the park?"

"We had to go to the funeral home. So many flowers have come in for Mom, of course, and we wanted to see those. I got a list so we could start thank yous while we're confined here." She frowned. "Then when we came back, they said at the gate that one of those men from Chicago was killed last night during the storm?"

Frannie thought she probably shouldn't reveal much. "I don't know if they have a time of death yet. Ironically, one of the last things he apparently did yesterday was order flowers for your mother. They had words on Friday night and he must have felt pretty bad about it."

Jodi looked puzzled. "Really? I didn't see any names I didn't recognize."

"His name was Randy Burton," Frannie said. She almost said Harry Beaton.

Larry returned from his errand just then and Dave shook his hand, again thanking him and apologizing for his helplessness.

"Glad to help. Would you like to sit awhile?" He gestured toward the array of lawn chairs.

"No, no," Dave held up his hand. "We just wanted to say thanks. We need to get back—my son will be arriving later today."

"Oh, that will be a help," Jane Ann said, but the way Jodi rolled her eyes behind her father said maybe that wasn't the case.

"Yeah. Darren's a good boy. Well, time to go, Jodi." He put his hand on her shoulder and firmly turned her back toward the host site. She turned and gave a small wave as they left.

Stephanie said to Larry when they had gone. "Did you talk to Sanchez?"

"Yes, he said thanks for telling him. He was pretty surprised that your husband was able to get to the campground with all the searching going on."

"Believe me, he knows trails in this park that the rangers probably aren't even aware of. Thanks for doing that. I think it's time to get River in the shower."

River whirled around from where he played on the ground with Buster. "Noooooo!"

Rob said, "I was just about to head there myself. Want me to take him along?"

"I don't need a shower!" River appeared to be on the verge of tears.

"River, go with Rob and take a shower and then I'll play some more Slap Jack with you, how about that?" Donna said.

"We need to teach him Chicken Feet too," Frannie said.

River perked up. "What's Chicken Feet?"

"Another game we play when we're camping."

He slowly got to his feet. "Mom, I'm going to go to the shower with…" He looked at Rob.

"Rob."

"Yeah, him."

Stephanie smiled. "Let's go get your towel and clean clothes." His face fell again at the mention of clean clothes.

"But—"

"C'mon. You'll miss out."

He dutifully followed his mother around the end of Shoemakers' trailer while Rob headed to his own.

"I'll meet you in the road!" River hollered after him.

"Okay, buddy!"

Jane Ann stiffly pushed her chair upright. "I'm thinking a shower sounds pretty good."

"Me, too," Frannie said. "I'll go with you since Larry won't let me out alone."

A few minutes later, they were following Rob and River up the road, although much slower because of Jane Ann's sore knee.

"Frannie, I'm not sure how you're going to cover this weekend in your scrapbook," Jane Ann said.

"I know. It may be a chance to use that 'Serial Killer' font. Seriously, this is pretty unbelievable. I'm also thinking it's odd that the funeral home told Sanchez that Randy had ordered flowers and Jodi didn't see anything with that name. Didn't Sanchez say he talked to the assistant?"

"I think so."

"That's the guy who gives me the creeps. You know —" She stopped stock still in the road. "I think the director, Bonnard, said the assistant, Joel is his name, is from Chicago. Maybe he and Randy knew each other?"

"Frannie, you sound like those people who say 'Oh, you're from Iowa? Do you know so-and-so?'"

"I know. But I don't think it's a coincidence. Stub said this trip was Randy's idea."

"Seems so complicated, though. Don't forget that Dave Schlumm was not a model husband. And he was pretty controlling just now with his daughter. I think I've heard that most murders are committed by a family member."

"But then what about Randy? It would be even more of a coincidence to have two unrelated murders in this park the same year, let alone weekend."

"I know." They reached the shower house and found the women's side empty. A half-hour later, refreshed and freshly attired, they gathered up their things and headed back to the campsite.

"I was thinking," Frannie said, "Dave seemed much more relaxed today. What if he did kill Maeve and Randy knew something, so last night he got rid of Randy and now he thinks he's home free?"

"Yeah, that's a lot simpler." Jane Ann laughed. "And the cooler or box? And the phone call you overheard?"

"I didn't say it explained everything."

"How about this? " Jane Ann started ticking points off on her fingers. "Maeve and Randy were having an affair which is why Randy had the idea for this trip, Dave caught them but Randy got away, the mystery box was Maeve's suitcase in which she had packed all her sequined cruise clothes to run away with Randy, Randy had to get rid of the suitcase and made the phone call to arrange for someone to pick it up, Dave caught him and killed him and took the suitcase and buried it under an old oak in the woods." She took a deep breath.

Frannie covered her mouth and started to giggle, glancing sideways at Jane Ann and losing all control.

"Jane Ann, you're incorrigible." She gasped, wiping tears from her eyes. "How long did it take you to come up with that?"

"Just seconds. I have a mind like a steel trap you know. These criminals can't pull the wool over my eyes," she said, cool and straight-faced. They arrived back at the campsite, and Jane Ann had to explain to their husbands why Frannie dissolved into fits of laughter every time she tried to talk.

"I think she's overtired," Larry said. "It's funny, but not that funny."

Jane Ann was indignant. "I thought it was pretty funny."

They had just settled again like a flock of birds quieting after a flurry of activity when Ranger Phillips stopped on his rounds of the campground. He still looked like his breakfast hadn't agreed with him and his nervousness of the day before was increased by a second death on his watch.

He started to thank them for their help that morning when the air was riddled with machine gun-like explosions. Everyone, including the ranger ducked and then peered around cautiously. A slow flush crept up from Phillips collar to his face as realization dawned.

"Firecrackers," he said and shook his head sheepishly. "I suspected those kids down there were up to something." He nodded back toward the campground entrance. "I'd better check it out." He headed back in the direction he had come from.

Frannie had her hand over her pounding heart and said to the others, "I know it's early, but maybe I should go take a nap." Everyone agreed. Donna put cards out on the picnic table in preparation for River's return. She even smiled sympathetically at Frannie.

Frannie climbed the steps into the trailer just as Rob and River came back from the showers. River still looked grubby, although he wore different clothes, and was jabbering excitedly about the firecracker noises.

"We had to stop at the playground afterwards," Rob said.

Frannie smiled to herself at the futility of trying to keep a five-year-old clean. She put away her shower bag and collapsed on the bed. The windows were open on both sides of the little bedroom and a fresh breeze moved the blinds almost hypnotically. She could hear River's delight as he slapped jacks, and apparently every other card, with Donna and Mickey but it did not keep her awake.

However, she was jolted out of her dreams a short time later by whispered voices coming from the back side of the camper, the side where Stephanie's pop-up was. It took a moment for it to even register in her sleep-addled brain where she was and what time universe she was in. Gradually the voices clarified.

"What's the matter with you, Steph? You narced on me?" She didn't recognize the voice but could guess.

"They told me yesterday I had to. Two people have died here—the cops aren't foolin' around," Stephanie said in a hoarse whisper. "And now you're wasted again

—whadya expect? Ow! Let go! I'm sure people saw you this morning anyway so someone was bound to tell."

"You are an idiot but we both knew that. Well, you're on your own, now. I'm outa here. I ain't goin' back to jail."

Stephanie didn't reply—she'd been on her own for a long while. The sounds of Trey's exit into the woods came through the open window. Frannie looked at her watch and was surprised that she had been asleep less than an hour because she felt quite refreshed.

She got up, straightened her clothes and splashed a little water on her face. Deciding she had consumed plenty of coffee, she grabbed a can of pop out of the refrigerator. Sort of a health move. Outside River yelled "Chicken Feet!" and Donna and Mickey groaned. When she got outside, River was bouncing on the picnic bench pumping his fists in the air. Mickey and Donna each had about a dozen dominos in front of them while River was down to two. He looked at Frannie, a wide grin splitting his face. "I'm winning."

"Yes, but look at the competition."

"What do you mean?"

"Nothing…just joking. You're doing great."

"I know," he said and made his next play.

"He changes the rules in the middle of the game," grumbled Mickey.

"Well, suck it up," Frannie said. "You've been doing that for years."

"That's different."

Larry was stretched out on his lounger, looking at a golf magazine. "You didn't sleep very long."

"I know, but I feel a lot better."

"No more hysterics?" he said. "With everything else going on, we don't need the guys in white coats picking you up. Who would fix my supper?"

Stephanie came around the end of the camper, looking a little pale.

"Trey was just here."

"I heard him, Stephanie. I was inside."

"The jerk. He was out of it but I don't think he'll be back."

"Mom! I'm winning!" River called from the table.

Stephanie nodded at her son with a weak, but encouraging smile.

"Stephanie, is it possible that Trey was involved in a drug deal here in the park?" Frannie asked.

She folded her arms and shrugged. "Anything's possible. I'm sure he was high when he was here and he'll get the stuff anywhere or way he can."

Larry looked at Frannie and sat up in his lounger. "I think I'd better talk to Sanchez again."

Frannie agreed. "Maybe they could have someone patrol by Stephanie's site more often."

"Or just move Stephanie and River somewhere safe. This is not a good situation. I'll be back."

"I really don't think we're in danger, because Trey's scared—he plans to get out of here," Stephanie told Frannie after he left.

"There's no sense in taking chances, Stephanie."

"I suppose."

149

They wandered over by the frantic Chicken Feet game in time to see River skunk Donna and Mickey.

"Okay, River. Time to leave these nice people in peace," Stephanie told her son.

"It's no problem," Jane Ann said, propped up again in her lounge chair. "We're always glad for Mickey to have someone his age to play with."

Mickey looked crushed. "How can you say that?" But he ruffled River's hair and said to Stephanie "How about Rob and I take him over to the playground for a while?"

Stephanie only hesitated a moment. "I'm sure he'd love it. He thinks I restrict him too much."

Frannie said, "That's because you have more sense than those two."

Mickey started picking up the dominos. "I don't know how I tolerate this abuse. Where'd Larry go?"

Frannie told them about Trey's visits and Stephanie's suspicions of his condition.

"Wow. That's kind of scary," Donna said.

"That's why Larry went to talk to Sanchez again."

"So maybe this whole thing revolves around Randy and Stephanie's husband and a drug deal?" Rob asked.

"Who knows?" Frannie shrugged. "Dave Schlumm isn't out of the picture yet either."

"It could be Maeve's infidelity..." Jane Ann started but Frannie shushed her. "Don't go there. Larry will send me back for another nap." They all laughed and Rob and Mickey took off for the playground with River bouncing around like a rubber ball and asking, "Will you go down the slide again, Rob? Can we build a sand castle? Will those other kids be there?"

Stephanie shook her head. "Those guys are gluttons for punishment."

"Like I said, they don't have much sense," Frannie said.

Jane Ann suggested a game of Bananagrams and the women took over the table space recently vacated by the dominoes. Stephanie proved to be a whiz at word formation and skunked the other three twice. They were turning over the tiles for a third game when an unfamiliar car moved slowly through the campground driven by a young man they also had never seen.

"Wonder who that is," Donna said.

"Maybe Dave Schlumm's son? He's supposed to be arriving today," Frannie said.

They played another game with Jane Ann winning and decided to quit and move back around the fire.

Larry returned and reported on his visit with Sanchez and the sheriff. "The sheriff wants to move you and River to a motel. He doesn't trust your husband — too long a record," he said to Stephanie.

She got up reluctantly. "I'd better go pack some things and fix some lunch for River. Thanks again for everything."

Mickey and Rob returned soon after and left River with Stephanie at her picnic table. When they were seated around the fire, Mickey said, "Some fireworks at Schlumm's trailer." He picked up his book.

Jane Ann looked at him. "Well? What's the rest of it? Don't leave us hanging."

Rob jumped in. "A young guy, I guess it's Dave's son, arrived while we were at the playground. Right before we left, we heard Dave yelling at his daughter."

"I got a strong impression from the look on Jodi's face earlier that there might be some sibling rivalry going on," Frannie said.

"Maybe Dave favors the son, but it's the daughter who's nearby and shoulders most of the responsibility," said Mickey.

Everyone looked at him. "That's pretty perceptive and deep for you, Mick," Larry observed.

Mickey shrugged. "I'm more perceptive and deep than most people think."

"At the risk of sounding like sibling-in-law rivalry, that wouldn't be hard," Larry couldn't resist.

"Here we go again." But Jane Ann didn't get a chance to finish with another threat. Car doors slammed from the direction of Schlumms' trailer and seconds later the car that had arrived earlier went by at a little faster speed. Dave Schlumm's son drove and Dave was in the passenger seat, but no sign of Jodi.

"Well," Frannie said to the others, "the only thing normal about this weekend seems to be meals and I think it's time for lunch."

CHAPTER THIRTEEN

EARLY SUNDAY AFTERNOON

AFTER LUNCH THE WOMEN resumed their seats around the fire, more for the semblance of normalcy than the heat. The men decided to see if they could get the golf tournament on TV in Mickey's RV.

"I really feel sorry for Stub," Donna said looking across the road. "He didn't bargain for all this and now has lost a friend regardless of that friend's culpability."

Frannie nodded, somewhat surprised at Donna's sudden display of sensitivity and noticed what Donna already had, that Stub was back outside, sitting in a lawn chair, head down. None of his other friends were outside. She said to Donna "I think I'll go over and visit with him. Want to join me?"

"Sure."

"You just don't want me to go because you're afraid I'll ask him about Randy's affair with Maeve," Jane Ann said.

"Well, you're also laid up, but you're right. You can't be trusted."

As they approached, Stub looked up and his face brightened slightly. They pulled up chairs on each side of him and sat down.

"Hey, Stub. How're you doing?" Donna asked.

He just shook his head at first and then looked at each of them. "The more I think about it, the less I can believe it."

"How did you guys come up with this trip, anyway?" Frannie said.

He sat back in his chair and ran a hand through his thinning hair. "Randy said he wanted to come see these caves—'course we didn't know they were closed— and thought several of us ought to get a motel. I watched a dumb movie one night about traveling in an RV and thought, 'Hell, nobody's that stupid. We could do better than that. And why not make a big trip of it?'" He gave a wry smile. "Shows you what I know. It kind of grew from there."

"It's certainly a trip for the books," Donna agreed.

"If it will make you feel any better, Stub, all of the mishaps that have happened to you this weekend with this motorhome have happened to at least one of us," Frannie said and then added, "Just usually not all on the same weekend." That at least got a smile from him.

Donna said, "What do you do when you're not out on these adventures?"

"Believe it or not, I'm a social studies teacher."

"No kidding?" Frannie said. "I was too—retired now. What level?"

"High school juniors, American History. You?""Eighth grade, but also American History."

Stub smiled again. "Wow, junior high. That takes a lot of guts."

"I planned to teach high school but the only jobs available were in junior high. I grew to love it, but of all the people I taught with, I never knew anyone who started out wanting to teach that level."

Stub laughed. "So right." He sighed. "I've not been out west much and was really looking forward to taking some photos and picking up materials to use in my classes."

"Maybe that's something you need to do in a smaller group," Donna suggested.

A car pulled up and Joel Marner got out. He walked toward them and offered his hand to Stub. "Mr. Berger?"

Stub stood and took the hand. "Yes. And you are — ?"

"Joel Marner. I work for the local mortuary. I'm very sorry for your loss. The sheriff thought I should come and pick up Randy Burton's personal things and we can arrange to get them to his family."

Stub was confused. "I thought the county would be handling Randy's body. We can return his things to the family."

"You're right, but we will arrange to transport the body back to Chicago after the autopsy is done."

"Won't the sheriff and Agent Sanchez want to look through Randy's stuff for clues to his murder?"

Marner folded his arms and took a determined stance. "They can do that just as easily at the funeral home. This was the sheriff's idea."

"I don't know. I think I'd better talk to Sanchez first."

Marner's face turned a little red but he tried to stay cool. "How about this? We go ahead and gather up his stuff and meanwhile someone can call Sanchez. I won't take it without his say so."

"Well, I guess that would be okay." Stub turned to Frannie. "I hate to ask another favor but do you think your husband would contact the agent for me and see what he says?"

"No problem," Frannie said pulling out her cell phone. Marner gave her a quick look and she could see a little panic in those baby blues. He's up to something, she thought.

"Okay…thanks. I need to get started and get back to the funeral home for a visitation this afternoon." He looked at Stub. "Can you show me where his things would be? I have a box in the car."

Stub nodded, waited for Marner to get the box, and led him into the motorhome. Frannie tried to think of a way to stall Marner but was sure Stub would keep a close eye on him. So she called Larry's number and quickly told him what was going on.

"Okay, I'll call Sanchez and then come over."

He hung up and called back a minute later.

"He says to hold that stuff and he'll be there soon."

"I'll tell him, but I don't think he'll go along easily."

"I'll be there in a minute. Don't do anything foolish!"

"You know me..." Frannie started to say but her husband interrupted.

"That's what I'm saying." He hung up.

Donna said, "Is the agent coming?"

"Yes, but I need to slow that guy down if I can." They headed for the motorhome. Frannie knocked on the door and heard a loud "C'mon in!"

The two women entered. Stub's four friends were sprawled on the couch and in the captain's chairs, watching a NASCAR race. Two of them were also on cell phones; one appeared to be playing a video game.

"Stub's back in the bedroom. Hey, Stub! Visitors!"

Stub poked his head out the bedroom door. "Did you talk to the agent?"

"Larry did and he said to not let Randy's stuff go. He's coming here."

Stub motioned them back. With the two large men already in the room, only Frannie could squeeze in, so Donna waited in what passed for a hallway.

Marner was taking clothes out of a drawer and putting them in the box. He appeared to be furtively checking the pockets as he did so.

"Agent Sanchez would like you to leave those things here," Frannie told him.

"Sure, whatever he says, I was just going by the sheriff's instructions," he said, but continued to add things to the box.

"Maybe we should all wait outside for Agent Sanchez," Frannie suggested.

"Well, I thought it would save me some time if I went ahead, and then when he lets me take this, I can just get back on the job." He gave her a stare that said 'Don't mess with me.' Somehow she doubted that getting back on the job was his biggest concern.

"Okay," she said but made no move to leave herself.

He finished the clothes and said to Stub, "Did he have anything else in here? Electronics?"

"The police already have his cell phone. I don't think he had anything else."

Marner frowned slightly at the news about the cell phone. He straightened up. "Well, you know, if the agent wants to take charge of this stuff, that's fine. Now that I've packed it, the sheriff can just drop it off at the funeral home if he still wants us to take care of it. I'd better be getting back." He looked at his watch and started out of the room. Frannie realized she needed to move or get mowed over. She reversed direction and motioned Donna out ahead of her.

When they all got outside, Marner headed for his car. Larry leaned on the car, arms crossed.

He said, "Agent Sanchez would like you to wait here."

Marner showed his empty hands. "I'm not taking anything. He knows where to find me. I have to get back to work." He walked around to the driver's side of his car and Larry moved away from it.

Stub leaned over to Frannie and said, not quite in a whisper, "I didn't tell him about Randy's duffle or shaving kit." Frannie noticed Marner gave them a sideways glance but started his car and proceeded to turn it around behind Ferraro's motorhome and head for the campground entrance.

"That was a quick exit," Larry said.

"It's pretty obvious that he just wanted to search Randy's stuff," Frannie said. "Larry, where was Sanchez? I assumed he was near the entrance but if he was, he should have been here by now."

"He went into town to talk to the sheriff about moving Stephanie."

In fact, it was another ten minutes before Agent Sanchez pulled up in his car.

"So where is this guy from the funeral home?" Sanchez asked.

"He took off in a hurry once he had finished looking through Randy's things. I think he was looking for something that he didn't find," Frannie said.

"Did he take anything that you know of?"

"I'm sure he didn't," Stub said. "I watched him closely. When I realized he was searching for something, I didn't tell him about Randy's duffel bag or shaving kit. Not that there's anything in them."

"Would you get all of his things for me, please?"

"Sure." Stub was soon back with the box of clothes, a large blue duffel bag, and a shaving kit and set them on the picnic table. Agent Sanchez checked through the shaving kit and then the duffel bag. At first the duffel appeared to be empty, but then he discovered a folded slip of paper in an inside pocket. He opened it while Frannie tried to discreetly peer over his shoulder.

He looked up and caught her. She backed up a step. "There's several addresses—Ortho Tissue Services in Lincoln, Nebraska, Bart Mische in Laramie, Wyoming and LaDonna Preston in Jackson

Hole. Are you going all of those places?" he asked Stub, pointedly ignoring Frannie.

"We were," Stub answered. "We changed plans after all this and are headed back to Chicago. Those must be people that Randy was going to look up on the way."

"Ortho Tissue Services?"

"I don't know!" Stub was exasperated. "Maybe he knows someone who works there."

"Maybe," Sanchez said.

Frannie said to Sanchez, "Can you tell if that's the same handwriting as the note we got last night?"

Sanchez shook his head. "No, but we'll check that."

"Marner said the sheriff told him to pick up Randy's things."

"That's what your husband said on the phone, so I asked Ingrham. He doesn't know anything about it."

"Agent Sanchez, another thing, Dave Schlumm's daughter didn't see any flowers from Randy. Didn't you say Joel Marner was the one who told you that?" Frannie asked.

He grimaced. "You're right; it was. I'll double-check with the director. First I need to talk to your neighbor." He crossed the road to Stephanie's pop-up. At the same time, the sheriff's car pulled up by Stephanie's campsite.

Sheriff Ingrham told Stephanie he would take her and her son to a nearby motel. It was decided to leave her pickup and pop-up where they were so that they would not lead Trey to Stephanie's whereabouts. River's dismay at leaving his new friends and potential domino victories abated somewhat at getting to ride in the sheriff's car. He waved vigorously as they pulled out.

They returned to their campsite. Mickey and Rob were back outside.

"Thought you guys were going to watch golf?" Donna said.

"Too much interference from the trees," Rob said. "Even Mickey's super-duper satellite won't pick it up."

"So you're stuck with us again?" Frannie said.

"What can we say?"

Donna suggested they walk down to see the bikers' tents. Jane Ann opted to continue resting her knee and Larry said he would stay for her protection, cleverly disguising that purpose by reading his golf magazine.

When they arrived at Richard and Elaine's campsite, they were given a necessarily short tour of the small tents. The other biker pair, Rog and his wife, a friendly woman with the improbable name of Peach, offered them iced tea. They sat in the fresh breeze of the lovely afternoon and pretended no one had died that weekend. Elaine told amusing mishaps from her days as a beginning farmer and Rob gave another detailed explanation of his lighting system.

They thanked the bikers for their hospitality and continued their walk to the end of the campground.

"This walk is becoming way too familiar," Rob said. "Only two days as a prisoner and already I'm verging on stir-crazy."

"Let's walk down to the youth campsite for a change of scenery," Donna suggested. They had just reached the path branching off the road.

"Just don't tell River that we went without him," Mickey said. The path wound down a hillside back into the woods about 150 feet and opened on a small level clearing. The clearing was shaded by a canopy of maples, ash and a few majestic shagbark hickory, and fringed by viburnum and western snowberry. Peeking from the understory, ferns and wild ginger carpeted the wooded ground. Flattened yellowed grassy spots around several fire rings betrayed recent tent sites. Frannie walked the perimeter, spotting several woodpeckers and a blue bunting in the woods. She returned to the picnic table where Donna sat.

"What a beautiful spot," she said.

Donna agreed. "It's hard to imagine what people first thought when they saw these places." A pause while she looked around. "'Course, I guess most of the world looked this way then."

"This spot, yes. The caves had to be somewhat unique, even then."

"Have you been to the old cabin Jane Ann talked about when we first got here?"

"Not for several years. It's pretty neat."

"Is the cabin open?"

"Not usually, unless they have something special going on. You can look in the windows, though."

Rob and Mickey had been examining the ragged bark of one of the hickories and walked back to the women.

"Neat place," Rob said. "Ready to head back? I feel a nap coming on."

"You men," Frannie told him with a grin. "You'll sleep your lives away. I feel just fine!"

Mickey hooted. "Not all of us got our naps in before lunch." They proceeded single file back up the trail, relishing the perfect breeze and intermittent dappled sunlight. Back on the campground road, they walked four abreast, stopping to visit with other campers.

When they reached the turn in the road and Dave Schlumm's camper, Jodi was just coming out the door, her arms full of clothes on hangers and a small suitcase. She glanced up at them and nodded, her eyes red and her face pale.

Frannie walked over to her and took the suitcase off her hands. "Jodi, what's wrong? Is there anything we can do?"

Jodi's shoulders heaved as she let out a big sigh. "It's my stupid brother. Whenever he's around, my dad goes all macho. I thought we should work on those thank you notes this afternoon and then have a quiet supper but Darren says if he had to come all the way back here—get that, because of his mom's death—he wants to see some of his old friends. So he and Dad decided to go to the tavern. I usually ignore their stupidity but this time I told them that would be disrespectful to Mom's memory. You know what Dad said? 'She's not gonna know!'"

"Oh, Jodi, I'm so sorry." Maybe Frannie was lucky that she had to handle her mother's death on her own.

Donna had followed Frannie. "But how did they get out of the campground? No one's supposed to leave."

"Oh, I'm sure they said they had to go back to the funeral home or something. But I really let them have it. Darren didn't even bring his family because it would have cramped his social life. Dad finally told me I'd better be gone when they came back!"

Now the tears were running down her face.

"Let us help you load your car and then come and have a glass of tea or something before you leave. Give you a chance to catch your breath," Donna said.

"Well…" Jodi hesitated and then gulped some air. "Okay, that sounds good."

They put her stuff in her car and while she went back to get her purse and lock the camper, they walked back to their own site, filling Rob and Mickey in as they went.

"What a couple of jerks," Mickey said.

Jodi moved her car down behind Ferraros' RV so that if her dad and brother returned before she left, they couldn't criticize her for still being at the Schlumms' camper. Rob went in to get the glass of iced tea. Frannie had just finished telling Jane Ann and Larry what had happened.

Jane Ann's mouth dropped open. "Larry, I promise I will never call you names again."

Jodi looked at them both more closely. "Are you brother and sister?" They both nodded. "And you camp together and everything?"

"That's because Frannie and Mickey are such good friends…" Larry said, but his wife slugged him in the arm.

"They'll never admit it but they're actually very close," Frannie said.

"That's great," Jodi said. "You don't know how fortunate you are."

"So, are you headed home?" Jane Ann asked.

Jodi nodded. "My son, Aaron, is home today and tomorrow. He has a summer job in a county park near Waterloo. He'll be a sophomore at Iowa State next fall in forestry. Mainly due to Mom's influence." She was quite proud. And Frannie thought again how little they knew of Maeve Schlumm based on what they had observed Friday night.

Jodi asked about their families and jobs and camping experiences. By the time she finished her tea, she had calmed down. "I'd better get going—I told Aaron I'd be home by supper time. He said he would take me out." She even beamed a little.

They said their goodbyes and wished her luck. She got into her car, adjusted her seat belt, waved and backed out.

The air was just cool enough that the campfire was welcome, and the group had plenty of wood to burn. Talk centered around the events of the day and the night before. Agent Sanchez, the sheriff and Deputy Smith were back going from campsite to campsite, questioning other campers.

Donna and Frannie filled the rest in on Joel Marner's strange and unprofessional behavior. Larry expanded on Trey's record of skirmishes with the law.

Rob, the accountant, said, "We need a spreadsheet to keep track of this mess. As I understand it, we've got two murders and at least four suspects and one person is on both lists."

"Both lists?" Mickey said.

"Randy," Larry said.

Mickey frowned. "Why would he still be a suspect in Maeve's murder? I don't see any connection between them."

Jane Ann sat up and barely opened her mouth when she received a withering look from her brother.

"You don't know everything," she said to him instead.

Frannie looked at Larry. "Remember this morning Sanchez said the most important problem in this case is motive?"

Larry nodded and Donna asked, "What did he mean by that?"

"Well, either both murders were committed by one person acting alone or something connects two or more of the suspects. On the surface, there doesn't appear be a real connection but motive would provide that. Dave and his wife are locals, retired, and campground hosts. Trey is local with a drug history and much younger. Even though Dave has had brushes with the law over domestic abuse, he's never been in trouble for drug use or even heavy drinking. And Stephanie told the agent that she and Trey didn't know the Schlumms other than to see

168

them here at the park. She claimed they had never even talked. "

Frannie picked up the thread. "Randy just intended to be here overnight and he's from the Chicago area. Joel Marner is also from Chicago but that's a big area and he's worked here a couple of months. So maybe there's a connection, maybe not. Today when he tried to get Randy's things, he didn't indicate that he knew Randy. I'm sure Stub didn't know him. And the funeral director just introduced Marner to Dave yesterday. "

"What about Marner and Trey?" Jane Ann asked. "They could know each other."

"Possibly. But not that anyone knows, not yet anyway. And there's always the possibility that someone else is involved that we don't suspect—or even know," Larry said.

"Seems like drugs could be a logical motive," Donna said. "It seems obvious that something illegal is changing hands—what else could it be?"

"Lots of things. Drugs are just the most common," Larry said.

"Don't forget the mysterious people in the Airstream," Jane Ann said. "What if the whole family is dead in there?"

Frannie said, "Jane Ann! Things are bad enough as it is." But they all looked down the road at the abandoned camper. It sat gleaming in its aluminum skin, sunlight reflecting off closed windows as well. All of the usual camping accouterments were stowed or missing. It was not telling any secrets.

"Why would someone tow a camper somewhere, spend one night, and then leave it sit the rest of the weekend?" Rob said.

"It's like the motives for the murders," Larry said. "There are all kinds of possibilities. Someone got sick, they had other plans for part of the weekend but wanted to hold their place, who knows?"

Sheriff Ingrham walked toward their circle just then and selected a lawn chair to collapse in.

"This case is sure getting me down," he said. "We don't often have a murder in this county, then to have two in one weekend in a place with people from all over — it's crazy."

"We were just talking about how crazy it seems," Frannie said. "Larry said you didn't ask Joel Marner to pick up Randy's things."

"I did not and as soon as I get back to town, I'll be talking to him. Nothing really adds up. None of these people seem to have any connection with each other. Wish I could figure out the motive — that ought to point to somebody." He looked at Larry. "Did you ever handle any murder cases?"

Larry shook his head. "Not like this. Perfection Falls is a very small town. We had a couple of killings over the years but more in the line of a knifing in a bar with twenty-five witnesses."

The sheriff said, "I still like Dave Schlumm for the murder of his wife—he didn't treat her very well. But that doesn't explain Randy Burton." Larry glared at his sister who pantomimed locking her lips and throwing away the key. "Better get back to town and see what this Marner has to say for himself." He got up to leave.

"Sheriff," Rob said, "On another note, we haven't seen any news. Was there a tornado last night?"

"Actually, yeah, one touched down south of here and took an old barn on an abandoned homestead. No damage other than that. We were lucky."

They all agreed and the sheriff left, heading down the road to his car. Everyone was quiet for quite awhile, mulling over events in their own minds.

Someone was bound to ask. This time it was Larry. "What's for supper tonight?"

"Pork chops," Donna said. "And a special surprise. We'll put them on in a couple of hours."

"Excellent!" Mickey said and picked up his book.

CHAPTER FOURTEEN

LATE SUNDAY AFTERNOON

FRANNIE GOT OUT OF her chair and stretched. "Potty trip," she said. "Who wants to chaperone?"

Donna jumped up. "I need to go too." Frannie cringed inwardly, but smiled and nodded. She was spending a lot more one-on-one time with Donna this weekend than she had planned. They started up the road together.

Donna said, "What a waste of a beautiful day. Doesn't it just drive you crazy that we're stuck here and can't go anywhere?"

Frannie shrugged. She realized that her instinct was to disagree with Donna, whatever her real point of view, but she was getting a little antsy herself. "Not crazy, but it is a little frustrating. We spend a lot of weekends, though, without leaving the park. We're more likely to find something outside the park if the weather is bad."

Donna looked at her, disbelieving. "Sometimes you never leave?" she said.

"Right. We mainly hike or do a little geocaching and a lot of just relaxing."

Donna shook her head slightly but didn't say anything else. When they came out of the restroom, they stood for a moment and watched a few kids on the playground. Frannie glanced over her shoulder at the area behind the shower house to assure herself that no one lurked nearby with a cellphone.

Donna pointed at a little-used path leading into the woods behind the shower house. "Do you know where that goes?"

"To the old cabin that Jane Ann talked about."

"Is it very far?"

"No, not terribly. Why?"

"Let's walk down there." Donna sounded like a small child, begging for one more cookie.

"I should tell Larry."

"Oh, c'mon. What will it take—ten or twenty minutes? He won't worry in that time."

"Okay, but we won't be able to look around much."

"We can come back later to do to that. Rob would like to see it too, I'm sure. This will just be a little walk." She turned and headed to the path.

Frannie followed and they had to step cautiously to avoid protruding roots and ankle-twisting depressions.

"Doesn't look like this path gets used much," Donna said over her shoulder.

"Apparently not. We've noticed that, with all of the budget cuts in the last year or so, a lot of park trails have gotten overgrown."

After about ten minutes, they reached a clearing. The ground sloped up behind the cabin. Towering trees loomed over the cabin roof, some branches hanging down so far that they appeared to be about to pluck the roof off the little building.

Donna picked her way to one of the windows and peered in "Wow, it's only one room! But kind of spooky. "

"Yeah, pretty rustic," Frannie answered, rubbing her arms in the chill of the deep woods and looking around. Donna went around the corner to another window and then to the back. "Frannie, come here!"

Frannie hesitated, feeling uneasy, but Donna didn't sound alarmed, just surprised. When Frannie arrived at the back of the cabin, Donna pointed at a weathered wooden door buried in the side of the hill.

"What is that?"

"It's a root cellar, built by the first settlers. I think they used it for storm protection too. This place has suffered from lack of maintenance lately. It used to be better kept up. We'd better get back — they'll be wondering about us."

"Sure, but I'm going to bring Rob back here."

They returned to the front of the cabin and started back up the path. Frannie was in the lead this time but was concentrating on her feet and not falling on her face when Donna hissed, "Frannie!" She looked back to see Donna wide-eyed and pointing off to the right. Frannie caught a glimpse through the trees of a spectral figure in black sweatpants and hooded sweatshirt headed their way. He (she assumed it was a he by the size) did not seem to be aware of them but instead focused on his own footing. Frannie was not normally skittish but decided this was not the time to take chances.

She glanced to the left and noticed that the ground sloped down around a protruding limestone bluff. She motioned for Donna to follow, and as quickly and quietly as she could, worked her way down the slope. Because the path was along a ridge and the ground fell away on both sides, they were soon out of the sightline of the approaching figure. When they reached the outcrop, they ducked around the backside of it.

Frannie was just saying a little prayer of thanks that for once Donna was quiet when her companion erupted with a dainty sneeze, clamping both hands over her mouth and nose. Fannie peeked around the outcrop. The figure had reached the trail and peered around trying to locate the source of the sound. However, what made Frannie's heart thunk as she pulled back behind the rocks was the gun in the man's hand.

Donna tugged on the back of her shirt. Frannie turned. Donna was making animated gestures apparently meant to ask, "Can you see him?"

So Frannie nodded and mouthed, "He has a gun." Donna's eyes bugged and her face paled. Frannie took another quick look and whispered, "It looks like he's heading back the way he came."

Donna took a deep breath. "Let's get back to the path and the campground. Sorry I even suggested this."

Frannie shook her head. "He's armed, Donna. If we go back to the trail, he'll be able to see us again. We need to keep going around this little cliff and find another way."

Donna didn't argue. She was all too happy to let Frannie take charge. Frannie checked again around the outcrop and when she didn't see any sign of the man with the gun, crept along the cliff going away from the path and Donna followed.

Walking was tricky. The ground dropped away from the cliff and numerous loose rocks made footing difficult. The women scrabbled on all fours as often as they walked upright. Frannie stopped to catch her breath and Donna ran into her.

"This cliff curves away from the campground," she whispered.

"How are we going to get back? Frannie, you're so calm."

"Not really. My stomach's in my throat." She brushed a couple of insects away from her face. "Let's think a minute. I don't know this part of the park at all."

She looked around. The cliff they had been skirting appeared to form one side of a bowl, curving around to meet the hill behind the old cabin. With their backs to the cliff, the heavily wooded ground sloped away from them, but Frannie could make out a small ravine through the trees where the ground started to climb again. If she wasn't completely disoriented—and that was certainly in the realm of possibility—that climb would lead back to the old cabin.

They heard a scuffling noise above them and small stones rattled down the cliff a few yards to their left. A disembodied voice called "Who's there?" Frannie and Donna tried to flatten themselves against the cliff as much as possible. They looked at each other in alarm, frozen with fear. Footsteps shuffled along the cliff top in their direction and then away again.

Finally, the footsteps indicated their stalker was moving away from the cliff back toward the trail.

"He's trying to find a way to get down here," Frannie said, her palms wet and fingers tingling.

"I thought you saw him go the other way?" Donna croaked.

"He must have circled around. He knew someone was out here. Here's what I think we should do. First, do you have your phone?"

Donna shook her head. She looked miserable.

"Crap. Me neither. All right, let's head down the hill—I think if we keep going that way, we'll get to the cabin. Then we can get back to the campground on the other side of the trail."

Donna nodded her head eagerly. All she heard was 'back to the campground.'

Frannie listened a few seconds and was satisfied that the noises from above were still going away from them. She started down the slope and mumbled back to Donna, "Be careful. The last thing we need is for either of us to sprain an ankle."

They threaded their way around fallen trees and thickets of brambly-looking shrubs. When they reached the bottom, Frannie took a quick survey back at their route. She couldn't see or hear anything unusual and started up the hill, she hoped toward the cabin. In places, the ground was so steep that they had to hang on to roots to make progress.

Part way up, they heard crashing sounds coming from the slope they had just descended. Frannie glanced over her shoulder and glimpsed their black-shrouded nemesis starting down.

Donna saw him too. "He'll shoot us!" she gasped.

"Not unless he gets a clear shot," Frannie panted as she sped up her pace—and she hoped she was right. "They would hear it in the campground."

Donna groaned and stubbed her toe. "Oof! That's reassuring."

A squirrel scrambled out of their way and raced up a tree where he scolded them roundly for invading his space.

They stumbled and clutched their way up the slope. Frannie grabbed a branch and felt a thorn pierce her palm.

"Ow!" She stopped and checked the wound, then kept going thinking: 'if he shoots us, I won't need a tetanus shot,' and: 'I'm too old for this.' Donna stumbled going over a branch and ripped the knee of her jeans.

"I should…know better…than to wear…my best ones camping," she gasped as they continued the climb.

As they neared the top, Frannie stopped and said, "Listen!"

Donna bent over, catching her breath. "I don't hear anything."

"That's just it. I think he quit following us."

"Oh my God, that was scary." Donna straightened up. "I didn't think we were going to get away from him."

"It isn't over. He's probably circling us again—going to try and cut us off."

"Oh." Donna sagged. "Now what?"

"I don't know. We could back track. He might not expect that."

"He could be just waiting for us though."

Frannie had to admit that was a possibility. "We're not far from the cabin. We can either hide there or at least find something to use as a weapon."

"Against a gun?"

"I don't know, Donna—we just have to do what we can." They got to the cabin without any more sign of the stalker. They checked the front door. There was a latch with a padlock, but the wood had rotted around it and the screws were rusty. Frannie was able to pull one side of the latch out and the door swung open with a screech. They hurried inside and looked around.

"Well, there's no hiding place in here," Frannie said looking around at the one room and spare furnishings. The rope bedstead had no mattress or linens and the table and chairs were of the simplest primitive construction that offered no concealment whatsoever.

Donna pointed above the large fireplace where a cast iron poker hung "What about that?"

"Yes!" Frannie said, but neither of them was tall enough to reach it.

"Where's Jane Ann when we need her?" Frannie said, pulling one of the chairs over to stand on. It looked sturdy but emitted a protesting crack as she climbed on. It held; she grabbed at the poker but it was fastened to the wall to prevent theft. She wrapped her hands around the rod, skinning her knuckles. She stepped off the chair into space, and her toes barely skimmed the floor so that her weight was enough to pull the fastener out of the brick on the right side and break the hooked end off the left side. She dropped on her feet falling backwards. Donna, who had been watching out the window, caught her and helped her right herself.

"Thanks," Frannie said. "You probably saved me from six broken bones." She let go of one end of the poker with her sore hand and licked her palm. It felt like it was on fire.

"I don't see anyone out there yet," Donna said.

Reaching down and grabbing the broken hook end as well, she said to Donna, "Let's get out of here before he does come back."

After they left the cabin and closed the door, Donna shoved the loose latch back in so that it wasn't obvious that anyone had been inside. Frannie put the iron hook end in the cargo pocket of her pants—so that's what those were for—and carried the rest of the poker in her uninjured hand. They prepared to go into the woods on the opposite side of the trail when they again spotted the man coming that very way.

Frannie grabbed Donna's hand. "Quick! The root cellar!"

They ducked around the back of the cabin and ran to the door in the hillside. There were no fasteners or handles, so Frannie pried her fingers under the bottom edge. It was heavier than it appeared and when they got it open together, they could see why. The inside had been reinforced with steel to preserve the door but maintain the authentic look on the outside. Four wooden steps led down into a small, squared off hole in the ground. Donna went down the steps and Frannie reached over and tried to pull some weeds and loose brush partially over the door as she closed it.

Donna said, "That won't hide it."

"I know, but maybe it will look like it hasn't been disturbed. Best I can do on short notice."

Frannie descended the steps and got a glimpse of wooden shelves lining the back wall. As they lowered the door into place, they heard the intruder come out of the woods into the clearing. Then they were in the darkest dark Frannie could ever remember.

They both stood stock still, barely breathing, and heard the screech of the cabin door, clomping footsteps on the wood floor, and the door opening again. In spite of the heavy door, they thought they could hear footsteps passing outside. Then it was quiet. Frannie listened so hard it made her head hurt. As they stood, she became aware of cobwebs hanging off the wood reinforcement of the ceiling. And the possible other inhabitants of this little hidey-hole. Crawling things. Flying things. Frannie feared bats more than almost anything else. Except the guy outside...

Donna whispered in the dark, "I am so sorry. I even had fresh sweet corn as my surprise for supper." Her voice caught in a little sob.

Frannie smiled. Amazing what we worry about at times like this. "They won't eat it without us."

"It's not that...oh, I don't know what it is but it just makes me sad."

The silence returned. They strained to hear anything outside. Frannie shifted her weight and consciously unlocked her knees.

"Do you want sit down?" Donna asked.

"No! I mean, no—I'm fine."

"Neither of us is fine."

Good point, Frannie thought. She pushed the glow button on her watch. 5:30. What time had they left the campsite? She didn't know and asked Donna if she remembered.

"Maybe 4:00? Or 4:30? Why, is it important?"

"I'm sure Larry would start looking for us as soon as we were gone half an hour."

"Rob too."

"It's 5:30 now."

They stood listening again. To silence. Frannie felt a stiffness creep in and shifted a little again. Donna did the same. After many minutes, Donna whispered, "Could you tell who it was?"

"Not by sight, but I think it may be the mortician's assistant—Joel Marner."

"But why? Do you think he's into drugs?"

"No. I've thought about it since we talked about motive earlier. This is just a guess, but it was something you said yesterday."

"Me?"

"I said he gave me the creeps because he smirked about Maeve Schlumm's wish to be cremated and you said maybe he was a body snatcher."

"I was joking. Body snatchers would be upset about cremations."

"Not if they are stealing body parts. They usually do that when cremations are planned and they don't have to worry about open caskets. I saw a report on the news several months ago. I think Randy was a courier to deliver body parts that Marner had removed from bodies that were due to be cremated."

"That's kind of a stretch."

"It would be, but remember the address list Sanchez found."

"The tissue service."

"Exactly. It all fits. I think that's what Marner keeps coming back for — anything Randy might have written down about the delivery."

"But then, why was Randy killed?"

"Haven't figured that out — falling out among thieves?"

A sudden crunch above their heads and blinding light as the door was wrenched open made them jump and squeeze their eyes shut at the same time.

"Ladies. I know you're camping but aren't these accommodations a little too rustic?" The black hood shrouded most of the face but the marble blue eyes identified Joel Marner and the gun in his hand belied his friendly greeting. Somehow, Frannie didn't feel any better about being right on his identity. "Out." He used the gun as a traffic cop wielded a nightstick and seemed bigger than life, both by virtue of his much greater height and being poised several steps above them.

Frannie pushed Donna lightly in the back to go up first and held the broken iron poker down alongside her leg with her left hand. Donna hesitated and looked at her uncertainly but when Frannie nodded, climbed the few steps. Marner motioned Donna to his side and Frannie to come up.

When she did, he couldn't watch both women at once and Frannie knew this was possibly her only opportunity to use the poker. But—and it was a big 'but'—, he could get off a shot or the gun could fire accidentally or if she didn't put him totally out of commission, he could retaliate. These possibilities went through her head in a split second, but caused her to hesitate too long.

"What's in your hand?" he demanded and at the same time out of the corner of his eye saw Donna start to edge away. He swung the gun toward Donna without taking his eyes off Frannie.

"Drop it, or she's dead. I have nothing to lose."

Frannie dropped the poker on the dirt floor of the cellar and climbed the steps to stand beside Donna. He motioned them to move out of the clearing along the base of the hill in the direction they had originally seen him coming from. As they reached the woods, so did the sound of distant yelling. Hope surged in each of the women as they heard their names being called.

"One peep and you're both dead. Like I said, at this point, I have nothing to lose. Now keep walking, straight ahead!" He nudged Frannie in the back with the gun barrel.

She couldn't help but think: One peep? I'm in an old movie! But the voices were getting nearer and though she couldn't see anyone yet, she was sure

Marner could not get them out of the park before the rescuers reached them. Would he start shooting if he was cornered? Or use them as hostages? She didn't know what to hope for.

Those thoughts fizzled like a burning match tossed in a pond when Marner ordered them to stop. As they had moved along the hill, it had morphed into another bluff. They stopped near a group of shrubs, and Marner said, "Get behind there." Frannie's brain scoffed at his futility until she realized the shrubs hid a small cave opening.

They had to stoop slightly to get in and then were able to stand once they entered. Marner, behind them, switched on a flashlight to illuminate the way. The cave was narrow but continued back into the bluff. The flashlight projected their shadows onto the cave walls in grotesque shapes. Frannie's hopes of rescue crashed and burned. Someone connected with the park service would be aware of this cave but not most of the rescuers. It could be hours before anyone would get around to searching here.

The cave was deeper than she expected. They had to climb over boulders and crouch down in places but it kept going, and she sensed in an upward direction. She was aware of fluttering above her head at times and moving shapes off to the sides. She knew what they were and the hollow of cold fear in the pit of her stomach grew until she felt she couldn't contain it. But they stumbled ahead, hands cut and bruised, knees screaming in protest. Her doctor had told her after a bone density test to be sure and stay active. Was this what he had in mind?

She tried to think positively. He hadn't killed them yet; she was sure he feared shots would pinpoint their location to the searchers. They outnumbered him, although the gun gave him an advantage she didn't want to think about. He hadn't tied them up, although he probably hadn't come prepared for that and besides, they never would have gotten through this cave if they had been restricted in any way. And lots and lots of people were looking for them. She wished she could convey these thoughts to Donna; she could hear her whimpering softly ahead.

They rounded a corner and got a glimpse of light up ahead. This was not just a cave; it was a natural tunnel through the bluff. Apparently, the light spurred Donna on because she moved faster. When they reached the opening, Marner said, "Stand right where I can see you." Donna did and Frannie stood beside her when she emerged. The soft evening light gilding the trees created a scene worthy of the finest pastoral painters. Frannie thought of all the similar evenings she had spent with friends and family at a picnic table, on their deck at home or around a campfire, not a care in the world.

Marner was right behind them and motioned them toward a gray delivery van parked a few feet away on a narrow dirt lane. The lane connected at right angles with a gravel road. He opened the back cargo doors and said, "Get in. Sit down on the floor, one of you on each side, facing the wall." They did as ordered, climbing in with some effort. The van was mostly empty except for a toolbox on one side near the back and some shelves along Frannie's side.

Marner slid the toolbox over and opened it with one hand, keeping the gun trained on them with the other. He rummaged through it and pulled out a roll of duct tape. So much for point three of her positive thinking.

Duct tape being duct tape, Frannie wondered how he was going to do anything with it and still keep the gun on them. She could feel the iron hook from the fireplace poker pressing against her leg.

Her question was answered when he said to Donna, "You! Get over here."

Donna got gingerly to her feet and moved toward him.

"Pull a piece of this tape out."

She took the tape and after fumbling to get the cut edge free, pulled about two feet out from the roll.

"Hold it up." He took a utility knife out of the toolbox and used his thumb to extend the blade. "Hold that tape still." Donna's hands were shaking at both ends of the tape and with effort she managed to steady them. Marner cut the piece of tape off the roll.

"Now, wrap that around your buddy's wrists." To Frannie, he directed, "Put your wrists behind you —quick!" He kept taking glances around the side of the truck at the road. Donna did as she was told, trying to keep the tape somewhat loose but Marner barked, "Tighter!" When she finished, he told her to come back and get another piece of tape. He then climbed up in the truck, instructed Donna to sit facing the other side, stuck the gun in his pocket and taped Donna's wrists tight enough that she squealed. He checked the tape on Frannie's wrists and satisfied, pulled a couple of rags out of a bin on the shelf. He wadded them up and stuffed one in each of the women's mouths.

The rags were clean but had the scent of being used for something oily in the past. Frannie realized why they were called 'gags' and concentrated on breathing through her nose.

Marner said, "Okay, girls, we're going for a little ride and what happens to you depends on how you behave. We'll be making one quick stop first. Got it?" He laughed and jumped out of the truck and slammed and locked the cargo doors. Soon they heard the truck start and it bounced along the rutted dirt road to the gravel. Both women fell over sideways at the first jolt. Frannie tried to ignore the jolts to her body by considering the possibilities. She could use her feet to rotate around to face Donna and somehow they could help each other. But if they stopped soon and Marner checked on them — which of course he would — he would bind them more securely and lessen their chances of getting free. Best to hold off. Above all else, she was sure he would not leave them alive.

CHAPTER FIFTEEN

SUNDAY EVENING

THE RIDE DID NOT improve. Lying on her right side, Frannie felt like that hip was being pounded with a ball bat. She had to constantly remember to breathe through her nose or she would choke. It didn't help that a very fine gravel dust found its way into the cargo area and filled her nostrils. They were separated from the driver's area by a bulkhead with a mesh screen at the top but, because of the angle, couldn't see Marner. After five or ten minutes, they bumped onto a smoother road and the bouncing lessened as well as the dust. A few minutes more and they came to an abrupt halt, sliding the women forward. The driver's door slammed and one of the cargo doors opened. Marner climbed in. Through the partially open door it was quite dark, which puzzled Frannie because she was pretty sure it wasn't later than 7:00.

He bent over each of them and checked their wrists and gags. "Back in a minute!" he said cheerfully and hopped back out, closing and locking the door behind him.

Frannie let a few quiet seconds go by and then used her feet to spin around a half turn. Scooting along the floor, she hoped she was getting closer to Donna. Frannie 'mmprhed' through her gag and listened for any response. She sensed that she was close and finally her head collided with Donna's back.

At first Donna didn't understand what Frannie was trying to do but then she realized her hands were touching the gag in Frannie's mouth. She grasped the gag with two fingers and tried to pull. However, she had no flexibility in her arms in her bound position so Frannie edged backward. Donna hung on and gradually the disgusting cloth emerged from Frannie's mouth.

The dryness in her mouth was almost debilitating but she managed to spit out, "I'm going to try and get my wrists loose. You taped over my watch, so that should help." Which turned out to be the case. She could move her old, cheap expansion band up and down slightly, adding a little give to the tape. Wiggling and squirming, she was able to get her left hand out. No time to enjoy the relief in her shoulders and arms, she left the tape on her right wrist and pulled her watch out of the hanging loop of tape.

Enough ambient light came through the mesh top of the bulkhead and her eyes had adjusted enough that she could see Donna curled in the fetal position at her feet. She leaned over first and removed the gag. Donna gasped and coughed while Frannie went to work on her wrist restraints. Marner had been more thorough on that task than Donna had been on Frannie and the removal took a little longer.

"What if he comes back before you're done?" Donna asked. The panic was apparent in her voice.

"Donna, we have to face that he is going to kill us. He can't leave us alive. The only reason he hasn't is that it would draw attention to him, so we're still somewhere

where that's likely. I think we're in town. So we have nothing to lose." She helped Donna to her feet.

"But now what? We're locked in here."

Frannie pulled the poker hook out of her cargo pocket. She could see that the bulkhead was fastened to the roof of the van with straps and bolts. A door in the center of the bulkhead gave access to the front of the van but it was locked. She hooked the end of the poker through the mesh and tried to use it as a lever. Someone should have paid closer attention in high school physics.

She managed a little leverage but the ancient wrought iron was brittle. Donna searched the mostly empty shelves on one side of the cargo area and said, "Aha!" Frannie turned around and saw Donna holding up a screwdriver. Between the two tools, they were able to pry the door open at the lock. They scrambled through the door, over the seat and out the driver's side door.

Frannie looked around. They were in a three-stall, high-ceilinged garage, softly lit by a security light near an interior door. At first, she thought it might be an apartment complex, but then she noticed the vehicle in the far stall was a hearse.

"We're in the funeral home garage," she told Donna. "Automatic door opener," she said looking up. Then she looked in the driver's side of the van. "Jerkface, of course, took the remote with him, but there should be a wall button near the entry door." They ran around the front of the van to the door leading into the home. There was no button on either side of the door—just light switches.

Donna pointed up to the opener. "There's the rope that's a manual override…" They both realized at the same time that only a short fragment remained and the end was too high to reach.

"Unless you want to stand on my shoulders, I think we're out of luck there. The button must be inside. I'm going in."

"Not alone," Donna said.

Frannie put her ear against the door, but heard nothing. She tried the knob. Not locked, so she slowly turned it, pulling the door open just a crack. It appeared to open on to a long darkened hallway. A heavy chemical smell hung in the air. She peeked around the corner and saw another long hallway at right angles to the first one. She didn't immediately see a control for the garage door, but at the end of that hall, was the beckoning promise of a red exit sign.

She didn't hear anything so motioned Donna to follow her. They both held their breath as they crept along the hall toward freedom. Diffused light was coming from a doorway about halfway along on the left. Frannie assumed it was another security light. When they reached the corner, she took a quick look around it to verify — and she was wrong. It took a moment to take in the scene before she let out an involuntary gasp.

The door opened on another short corridor. Through the door, she could see a second open door and, by an angled view into a brightly lit room, a table on which she could just make out the pale face of Maeve Schlumm and blocking the rest of Maeve's body, the back of Joel

Marner. On the floor at Marner's feet was an ancient green cooler that appeared to be filled with bones.

At her gasp, Marner spun around, a scalpel in his hand, and yelled "Hey!" Frannie turned and pushing Donna ahead of her back toward the garage, said, "Run!" Donna reached the juncture of the two hallways and dodged to the left rather than through the garage door as Frannie expected but probably a better choice. Too late she realized that they should have run toward the exit sign. Marner thundered behind them swearing and yelling. Donna opened the first door she came to and they ducked into a small room that was used to store sound equipment and extra chairs. Frannie slammed the door and pulled a chair over under the knob.

Donna had continued through another door into a chapel-like room, knocking over folding chairs as she went. Frannie followed her as Marner pounded on the door behind them, but pulled up short when the loop of tape still hanging on her right wrist caught on the door handle. As she struggled to free herself, she hissed to Donna, "If you can't find a door out, break a window!"

By the time she was loose, Marner had quit pounding on the door and his footsteps receded down the hallway. He must be circling, having the advantage of knowing his way around. The chapel room was divided from another large room with an accordion wall. Donna had ducked around the open end of it and Frannie followed.

Every room had the eerie glow of security lights and was heavy with the scent of funeral flowers. Another accordion partition created a third room. This one had a large heavy casket on a mobile stand at the front surrounded by huge baskets and vases of floral arrangements and lit from above by a subtle can light. Donna knocked over a vase as she tried to get around to a door on the other side. She righted herself but Frannie slipped in the puddle and went down hard.

As Frannie struggled to her feet, she heard a door open at the other end of the room and knew Marner was trying to head them off. She dodged back around the accordion wall to the middle room and searched for a hiding place or a way out. A miniature jungle of potted palms backed a podium and she could see light coming from behind them. A small angled corridor led to a wider hall.

She turned right and raced into an office reception area. Again she pushed the door closed and braced a chair under the knob. A light glowing on the desk caught her eye—a phone. She had just punched in 911 just as Marner started pounding on the door. She dropped the receiver on the desk and ducked out another door, hearing the phone squawk "Hello? Hello? Is this an emergency?" Well, maybe. Another short passageway took her back to the hall where they first had tried to make their escape. Marner now shook the office door and she had come full circle.

She knew the door to her right—the storage room—was blocked. Ahead, at the end of the hall was the door to the garage but that too was a dead end. She opened the door to the left and found herself in a room full of caskets. There were no windows but a small security light above the door. She closed the door quietly but there was nothing she could move to block it.

She had no choice. She had to hide in a casket. She chose one in the middle, thinking Marner would look first in the ones nearest the door and then think that she would have gone clear to the back. She hoped. They were all arranged with a closed casket on the bottom of a special stand and one with the half lid open on the top. The bottom ones could not be opened without pulling them out, so she would need to hide in the bottom half of a top one.

She used the bottom casket to climb up and into the one she had chosen as a hiding place and curled up under the bottom half of the lid. For once, she was grateful that she didn't have to deal with Jane Ann's height. There was a satin blanket which she tried to arrange to block the inside view, willing herself not to think about where she was. It was better than a root cellar with snakes and spiders. Or a cave with bats. Right.

Her heart pounded so loud that she was sure it could be heard all over the building. At which point she realized that she hadn't heard any outside doors opening or glass breaking or alarms that would indicate Donna had escaped. But Marner had followed Frannie—she remembered him pounding on the office door—so Donna should have been able to get away.

Her breathing was just getting back to normal when she heard the door open. She froze, hoping in a little part of her soul that it was Donna, even though that would mean that she hadn't escaped. But no one said anything and Donna surely would have called her name.

She could hear footsteps slowly circling the room, stopping as he checked each casket. Her hope collapsed that he would first check the ones farthest from the door. If Donna was getting help, every extra minute before discovery could be crucial.

He was getting nearer and she could hear him opening each bottom lid. Finally, she was sure he was at the one next to her hiding place and she froze with fear straining to hear any sounds of sirens or rescue. Nothing.

He lifted the bottom lid of her casket. She lay curled facing down so she couldn't see him and couldn't make herself look.

"Well, well. One of my little runners." He grabbed her arm and yanked her to sitting. "Where's your buddy?"

"She got away. She's getting the police," Frannie croaked.

"Right. We'll see about that. Get out of there!" He jerked her up and out, her foot catching and giving a painful twist to her knee. With a firm grip on her arm, he hauled her around the room, quickly lifting the other lids and slamming them shut.

"Why are you doing this?" Frannie tried to reason. "They'll know who you are without us. Why don't you just try to get away? I'm telling you, Donna got out of the building! We split up back there in that chapel."

He finished checking the last caskets in the room. "Your little detective antics interrupted my supply. I am leaving and you are going to help me replace some of that supply." He reached the door and pulled her through it. Frannie remembered the cooler full of bones and saw his plan. He dragged her down the hall and around the corner to the prep room where he had been about to work on Maeve Schlumm's body. Frannie struggled and dragged her feet to at least slow him down but he clamped down on her arm and jerked her upright. That he had not had time to mutilate Maeve's body was a small consolation, but she also realized who would pay the price for that.

She was exhausted from the ordeal, aching with the sharp pain in her knee, and could not continue to fight back. He closed the cooler of bones, grabbed his gun off the counter, and let go of her arm, using the gun to motion her out the door ahead of him.

"The garage—hurry up about it," he said, jabbing her in the back with the gun. "Open the door." She did as she was told and went down the three steps into the garage. When they got around the van, he looked at the open door and the mangled bulkhead. He glanced at her with almost a hint of admiration, but then pushed her up into the driver's seat and back through the busted door. With one hand he wrenched the door closed, jamming it worse than the padlock had, laid the gun on the passenger seat, and started the van. He reached in his left pants pocket and pulled out the door remote, hitting the button, and throwing the remote on the dashboard. The oversized door glided up.

Frannie watched him through the bulkhead mesh as he threw the van in reverse. She hung on as they started to move. Marner glanced in his side mirror and hit the brake. Frannie peered over his shoulder at the mirror.

Framed in the open garage door in the deepening twilight was a sight that lifted her pounding heart. Sheriff Ingrham, Deputy Smith and another officer all stood with guns trained on the van. Marner reached for his gun and swung it around to aim at the bulkhead. At the same time, he hit the window control and as it slid down yelled, "I have one of the women. Put those guns down and back away or she's dead!"

Frannie started to shift her position from the passenger side to directly behind Marner. He saw her in the mirror and ordered her to stay where she was, waving the gun for emphasis. Her hopes sunk as she peeked through the mesh at the mirror and saw the law officers lay their guns on the driveway and step back. Marner started to shift the van into reverse, still pointing the gun with his right hand back at the bulkhead and watching the officers in the mirror.

Suddenly, the passenger door was flung open and Larry, in a crouch, jack-in-the-boxed up to grab Marner's wrist and give it a twist. The gun went off and then flew out of his hand and the van. Joel's mouth dropped open as he swung his head around to see what had happened. Larry kept a grip on the wrist with his right hand while clutching his own shoulder with his left, his face twisted in pain. Frannie's stomach took another flop as she noticed blood oozing out between his fingers.

While Larry distracted and disarmed Marner, the officers retrieved their weapons and rushed the driver's side, wrenching open the door. Sanchez deftly reached under the steering wheel and turned off the key.

The sheriff and Sanchez pulled Marner from the vehicle onto the garage floor while Deputy Smith took the keys from Sanchez. Larry, still clutching his shoulder, called weakly, "Frannie?"

"I'm here," she pressed her face to the mesh. "I'm fine." She felt giddy — well, except for the bruises on her arm from Marner's grip, a thorn in her palm, scrapes on her knees, a twisted knee, bug bites, and other minor ailments. Just fine.

Deputy Smith unlocked the cargo doors and Frannie crouch-walked to the back where the deputy helped her out. Things were a blur for a while. She saw Donna on the driveway with Rob, but hobbled around the van to see to Larry. The deputy hustled them both into a squad car and drove them, complete with lights and sirens, to the small local hospital. On the way, Larry handed Frannie his phone with instructions to call Jane Ann and Mickey.

When Frannie hung up, she reported to Larry that Mickey was preparing a couple of his famous pizzas to cook on the grill for them when they got back to the park.

"Will I have to make a statement to the police yet tonight?" she then asked the deputy.

Linda Smith shook her head and smiled at them in the rear view mirror. "No, they'll get that from you tomorrow. You've had a big enough day. You know, you two look like a couple of teenagers."

Frannie looked at Larry and grinned. She sat tucked under his good arm, safe and content for the first time in a couple of days. "I guarantee you, the last thing I feel like tonight is a teenager. Every muscle and joint aches!"

Larry said, "The worst part is that they will all hurt twice as bad tomorrow."

Linda let them out at the hospital emergency entrance. They waved to her and turned to enter the hospital when a loud explosion sounded behind them. As they both whipped around to see, Frannie felt fear clutch her heart again. What she saw made her bubble over with laughter. In the dark sky, red, white and blue stars and glitter blossomed out from a center and drifted to the ground, replaced by a fountain of gold shimmer, and then a series of purple and green starbursts. She had forgotten it was July Fourth. Larry squeezed her shoulder — but in a different way than Joel Marner had — and they headed into the emergency room.

Larry's shoulder was only grazed, so the wound was cleaned and dressed in less than an hour. Frannie also had them look at her palm where she had grabbed a thorny branch. A little cleaning, antibiotic cream, and dressing took care of that. They came out to the waiting area to find Linda Smith browsing an old magazine.

She looked up, set the magazine aside and stood. "Ready to head home?"

They looked at each other. "You bet!" Larry said. Then he said to Frannie, "Wow. Your hair's a mess!"

"Yeah, well, you have a bullet hole in your favorite police marathon t-shirt."

Linda looked at him with interest. "You run marathons, Mr. Shoemaker?"

Larry started to concoct a story, but Frannie jumped in. "No, he bribes his friends to bring him t-shirts."

He grinned and said, "Right now I'm wishing it was a sweatshirt."

"I've got a blanket in the car," Linda said. "Let's get you back to that pizza."

As they followed Linda out, Frannie realized she was starving as well as grubby. They arrived back in the campground to a large welcoming party. Rob and Donna were already back; Stub and his friends had brought over extra lawn chairs, and the bikers, Rich and Elaine, Rog and Peach, had walked down to join the celebration. A cheer actually went up and applause sounded as they got out of the squad car.

"Hail the conquering hero!" Mickey shouted.

"Thanks," Larry said.

"I meant Frannie," Mickey said, whacking his brother-in-law on the shoulder, eliciting a wince. "Oops, sorry! Adding injury to insult. Not good, it's supposed to be the other way around. Sit over here—I have a beer with your name on it."

Larry said, "You're insane, Ferraro."

Frannie broke away from Jane Ann's hug and said, "I need to get Larry a jacket." She headed to the camper but was waylaid by Cuba hitting her in the back of the knees.

She bent to scratch her behind the ears. "Hey, old girl. You missed me?"

When she came back out, Cuba had found Larry and curled around his feet. She helped him into the jacket and turned to find Donna right behind her. She wrapped her arms around Frannie and said in a hoarse voice "I'm so glad you're okay! You saved my life."

Frannie shook her head, her eyes tearing up. "It was a team effort. I'd be history by now if you hadn't gotten away and called for help."

Donna smiled shyly. "I didn't have time to call. I broke a window and it set off a silent alarm. They were here soon after."

"Well, whatever. We made it and I wasn't very optimistic about that most of the time."

Larry said, "We have lots of questions for you two."

"First, I need a shower, much as I hate to miss any of the party."

"Me too, but are you sure you want to go back to the shower house?" Donna asked.

Larry interrupted. "I'm sending Jane Ann with you, sore knee or not. She will have her cell phone."

Frannie protested. "Larry, that's not necessary. I don't think there's any more bad guys roaming the park."

"Shut up, woman. It's not just that—she can call for help if one of you passes out in the shower."

Jane Ann nodded and said, "I'm going. No argument. Get your stuff."

Frannie said to Donna, "She's bossier than Marner." Donna agreed.

A half hour later, they returned to the party under Jane Ann's close supervision. Frannie felt better than she expected, clean and dressed in fresh jeans, a white t-shirt, and a yellow hoodie. She pulled a chair over next to Larry and realized that Agent Sanchez and Sheriff Ingrham had joined the group along with Ranger Phillips.

She looked around and relished the welcome familiarity of the fire-lit faces circling the campfire. Mickey sported his chef's hat, standard in his camping wardrobe, and shoveled the first pizza off the grill on to a waiting pan held by Jane Ann. She hobbled over, laid it on the picnic table with a flourish, and expertly cut it in squares. Plates were handed around, first to Donna, Frannie and Larry. Mickey started another one, and campers showered him with compliments, much to his pleasure.

"How are you doing, Mrs. Shoemaker?" Sanchez asked.

"Well, it was quite a ride," and seeing his expression she added, "I'm not being flippant. I can't believe everything that did happen and everything I thought was going to happen between the time we left the shower house and when you showed up at the funeral home. Not an experience I'd care to repeat."

"I'm sure not. We think we have most of this pieced together but we'll get your take and the full story tomorrow, okay?"

Frannie nodded. "There's a cave near the old cabin that actually is a tunnel leading to a road outside the park."

Sanchez said, "Your husband found that with Randy's GPS. Remember there were coordinates for two nearby sites. We only checked out the first this morning."

Frannie laughed weakly. "That was only this morning?"

"What about Stephanie?" Donna asked. "Will she be able to come back now that Marner's been arrested? It sounds like her husband didn't have anything to do with this."

"We think it's best that she wait until morning; then we'll bring her out to get her truck and camper. I don't think Trey was involved, but we don't know what else he's capable of — he did threaten her."

"Wow." Frannie was still overwhelmed. "You wouldn't believe how quiet our weekends usually are compared to this." She gazed down the road. "What about the people in the Airstream? Did you ever contact them?"

Sheriff Ingrham laughed. He had just polished off his pizza and threw his plate in the fire. "We heard from them this afternoon. His father had a heart attack up in Wisconsin and the whole family headed up there first thing Saturday morning. When he heard about the murders on the news, he called the local police department today. They'll be back tomorrow to get their equipment."

"I wonder if they have any idea what people suspected them of this weekend," Donna said.

"Probably not."

Mickey and Rob were passing out seconds on the pizza and gave Frannie two more pieces. She was halfway through the second when she almost nodded off. Her plate started sliding off her lap. Larry noticed and touched her arm lightly. Her head jerked back and she jumped and looked around, confused.

"Whoa, there!" Larry said. "You don't need whiplash on top of everything else. What say you and me turn into pumpkins?"

She nodded gratefully and after everyone warned them about bedbugs, etc., they headed inside.

Chapter Sixteen

Monday Morning

IN SPITE OF HER exhausting day, Frannie woke up the next morning about 5:30. The previous two days' events replayed in her head. Cocooned safely in the comfy bed almost negated the fear and uncertainty. After a while she rolled out, found her slippers and hooded sweatshirt, and fixed the first pot of coffee. She and Cuba went outside to a glorious morning. She felt sore and battered, but the peeking sun promised a better day and lifted her spirits. Her flannel pajamas and sweatshirt felt perfect in the morning chill as they took a short turn around the campground.

By the time they got back, the coffee was ready and she apologized to Cuba that dogs couldn't have the fragrant brew. Cuba cocked her head and looked at Frannie with her standard 'Why don't humans make sense?' look. Frannie stirred up the coals in the fire ring and put a couple more logs on. She explained that dogs weren't in charge because they couldn't make fire. Cuba wasn't buying it. Frannie sat in her camp chair, one hand wrapped around her steaming mug, one on the dog's head and watched the morning unfold.

The new logs caught and the small flames mesmerized her. A door opened and she looked across the road to see Donna come out with Buster. They walked over to the fire.

"How are you doing this morning?" Frannie asked her.

"It seems like a dream today or a movie we watched or something, doesn't it?"

"I know…I'm feeling the same thing. Help yourself to some coffee if you want."

"I will. I'd better take the puppy around or she'll report abuse."

When they returned, Donna got her coffee and pulled up a chair by the fire. For ten minutes or so, they just sat there, staring into the fire.

Finally Donna said, "Frannie, I need to confess. I wasn't honest with you the other night."

Frannie looked at her puzzled. "What?…I can't remember past yesterday."

"I know. But I told you that my parents passed away twenty years ago. It's a story I've even told Rob. But the truth is I have no parents. I was abandoned as an infant and grew up in foster homes. I had so many behavior problems, no one would keep me. The longest was a year. I don't know what you went through losing your mother because I've never had any family to lose." Her voice broke and tears ran down her face.

This time Frannie did take her hand. "Donna, I'm so sorry. I can't imagine what you have gone through either."

"Yesterday was just more of the same. If I hadn't insisted on walking to the cabin, none of that would have happened."

"And Joel Marner would probably still be loose and all of these people would still be under suspicion and Mickey wouldn't have made pizza."

Donna face broke a little into a smile.

"Donna, what happened to us was Joel Marner's fault, not ours. We weren't trying to meddle or play Nancy Drew or anything. We were just taking a little hike and not alone so we should have been fine. We've taken other walks this weekend and nothing has happened."

"Except for finding a dead body."

"Yeah, there's that."

"I don't know why he came after us."

"Me either. Maybe just because we ran. But if we had continued on the path, we would have met him and how could he explain being out here? He had just told us a short time before that he had to get back to work."

A voice came from behind them. "Oh look! A beautiful morning and a couple of beautiful chicks by the fire."

Frannie turned and smiled at her husband. "You mean us or Cuba and Buster?"

"Hmmm. I meant four beautiful chicks by the fire."

"Thanks."

"Buster will be offended. He's not a chick," Donna said.

"We've always had female dogs; therefore all dogs are female. Did either of you get any sleep?"

They both nodded vigorously. He pulled another log from the bin and used his fire poker to arrange the fire into a little teepee. It soon burned with a bigger blaze.

"Men and fires," Donna said to Frannie. "What is it, anyway?"

"It's because they can't have babies."

"It seems to me," Larry said, pouring a cup of coffee, "that even though no one would know it by looking at us, we've missed a couple of serious meals through all this nonsense. Weren't we going to have smashed potatoes one morning?"

"We planned it for yesterday but decided to hold it for this morning," Frannie said.

"What are smashed potatoes?" Donna asked.

"You bake potatoes either in the oven or the micro, smash them down with a spatula, drizzle them with a little olive oil and salt and pepper and put them in oven until they get a little crispy. Then, you top them with sausage gravy. It's a health food."

"Wow! Sounds like it. And you're right, Larry. I had marinated pork chops for last night and a little extra surprise—early sweet corn. Except the surprise was on us."

"How about this? The sheriff and Sanchez will be back this morning to grill you girls so I'm thinking we'll pack up and leave early afternoon—after we get home and unload, we can gather in our back yard tonight and polish that stuff off. I can just set the grill up there."

"Excellent idea," Frannie said. "Are you and Rob busy? I mean, since you'd have to bring the food?"

Larry looked hurt. "We would be providing the grill, the cooking expertise, and scintillating company. Don't we have some peanut butter and crackers we could contribute?" A little eye rolling from Frannie.

"We'd love to," Donna said. "What would we do with all that food, anyway?"

"Settled, then. One thing decided for today."

Frannie said, "I think we have lots of salads left too."

"What's settled?" Mickey said, bouncing down the steps of his motor home brandishing an empty coffee cup.

"We're having last night's supper on our deck at home tonight."

"Excellent. And what's for breakfast and lunch?"

Larry said, "Get some coffee, sit down and shut up, Mick. We'll tell you when you need to know. And it wouldn't hurt if you made your own pot of coffee this morning instead of mooching ours."

"I'm hurt. We made a pot yesterday."

"Right. And this is our third morning here."

"Yeah, but—"

"Why don't you two go sit in our camper and argue? You could wake Rob up so you'd actually be accomplishing something," Donna said. Frannie high-fived her.

Jane Ann emerged at that point, gingerly descending the steps.

"Good morning all."

"It was until Larry got up all grouchy," Mickey said.

"I wasn't grouchy until I saw Mickey's face, was I, girls?"

"Ohmigosh, I'm going to call the sheriff and have him send Marner out here and lock you two up," Frannie declared.

"Are they being bad boys?" Jane Ann asked.

"No worse than usual," Frannie said.

"Okay, no sausage gravy and potatoes," Jane Ann said.

"I'm going to go make another pot of coffee," Mickey said, now contrite. "Larry, old buddy, can I get you anything? Wash your feet? Brush your teeth?"

"Done, but thanks for asking. Change of subject. Time for questions. What were you chicks doing yesterday?"

Donna said, "My fault. When we came out of the bathroom, I asked Frannie where that path went and she said to the old cabin. So I suggested we just walk out there and back. Dumb idea, as it turned out."

"Where did you run into Marner, at the cabin?"

"No," Frannie said. "We had just started back and saw him cutting through the trees. We would have run into him if we kept going so we ducked off the path the other way but he must have heard us."

"Did you know it was him?"

"No, it was just a guy all in black and he had his hood up and just seemed like he was sneaking around."

"And then when he got to the path, we saw he had a gun!" Donna said.

"So then what?"

"We were going to cut through the woods to get back here, but on the north side of that path, there's a bluff and we couldn't get around it so we went back to the cabin."

Rob had ambled across the road to join them. "Hold it, don't go any farther until I get my coffee. I want to hear this, too." In a few minutes, they were all back around the fire, including Mickey who had plugged another pot in.

"So you're back at the cabin," Larry said. "Not much place to hide there."

"We broke in," Donna said, "but you're right, there's no place to hide. So Frannie got the fireplace poker down from over the fireplace. We thought maybe we could use it as a weapon."

"It busted — the point thing came off," Frannie pointed to the similar one in Larry's hand, "so I put that in my pocket." She went on to describe how they hid in the root cellar, and Marner's discovery of them.

"I wonder why he even bothered looking for you," Larry said.

"Because we're cute chicks?" Frannie suggested.

"He must have thought we could identify him," Donna said. "Frannie mentioned this morning that we had just seen him at Stub's RV a little while before and he said he had to get back to the funeral home for a visitation. I don't think most funeral directors wear black hoodies to visitations."

"I think he wanted to shoot us then and there but was afraid someone would hear and know where he was. He saw the poker and made me drop it but I still had the point in my pocket. When he took us to that cave-tunnel, we could hear you guys calling us. I almost cried," Frannie said.

"That was Larry singing—that's why you wanted to cry," Mickey told her.

"Potatoes and gravy," Jane Ann said, and Mickey shut up.

Donna continued the story about the journey through the tunnel and being confined in the truck.

Frannie added, "He couldn't hold the gun on us both and tape our wrists at the same time so that was a lucky break. He made Donna do mine and we were able to get my watch in it and keep it a little slack or I never would have been able to get loose later."

"Why did he go to the funeral home? Why not just take off?" Rob asked.

"Maybe Sanchez will be able to tell us more, but I'm guessing he thought if he had to cut and run, to make one last effort to add to his bone collection."

"That's what I want to know," Mickey said. "What was he doing with the bones?"

"That's what this was all about, I think," said Frannie. "Several months ago, I saw a news report about the black market in human tissue. Not only organs, as you might expect, but everything else as well. Human bones are used in dental implants and orthopedic transplants. Theoretically they come from people who have willed their bodies to such purposes and have been screened for diseases. But when a body is scheduled to be cremated, it offers an opportunity to unscrupulous body snatchers who rob a corpse of its bones and maybe even replace them with plumbing pipe. Seriously. But because of the cremation, the family is none the wiser. These bones sell for thousands of dollars on the black market."

"Do you mean the funeral home was in on this?" Jane Ann asked, appalled.

Frannie shook her head. "No, I'm sure it was just Marner. Randy was a courier; one of the addresses Sanchez found in his things was for a tissue service in Nebraska. Stub said Randy was the one who suggested this trip, who wanted to stop at this park, and who didn't want to turn around in spite of the obvious fact that he wasn't enjoying the trip. It was supposed to be a simple pick up but Maeve Schlumm stumbled on to it."

"But why was Randy killed?" Mickey said.

"Wait!" said Rob. "We can talk about that later. Why did Marner go back to the funeral home?"

"He knew Maeve's body was there and going to be cremated. He probably felt she owed him for screwing up what for him was a lucrative set up. I think he was going to remove some of her bones to add to the ones he would now deliver. And I think he planned to do the same with us — that's why he took us along."

Donna's jaw dropped and her eyes grew wide. "Are you kidding me?"

Frannie shook her head. "'Fraid not."

"So he left you guys in the van to get Maeve's bones…" Rob prompted. Frannie explained how they got out of the van and why they had to go into the funeral home. "It's a big place," she said, "and fairly new. There's a large room in the center that can be divided into three big rooms for services or viewings. All the way around that is a hallway, with offices, storage rooms, prep rooms, et cetera around the outside. It's almost a maze. So we had a big disadvantage because he kept circling and cutting us off."

Donna told how they got separated, and Frannie finished the story with her account of hiding in the casket room.

"Wow." Jane Ann said when she finished. "You guys are amazing. I would have dissolved in tears at the beginning and that would have been the end of it."

"No, you wouldn't," Donna said. "Frannie was so calm, I couldn't believe it. She kept me from falling apart."

"It was mutual. So your turn to fill us in," Frannie said to Larry. "Were you already with the sheriff?"

"We had been ever since you disappeared. We already suspected Marner, of course, and when the alarm sounded at the funeral home and the 911 call came in about the same time, we headed there. We were just debating the best way to go in when that garage door opened. A stroke of luck."

"You know what they say, better to be lucky than smart," Rob said.

"In this case, definitely!" Larry agreed.

Mickey got up and refilled his coffee. "So how much longer do I have to behave myself? In other words, when are we going to eat?"

Jane Ann glared at her husband. "After all they went through, all you can think about is your stomach!"

"Mickey's right. We're going to waste away unless we get some sustenance. I'll get the potatoes going," Frannie said. "Maybe we can get breakfast out of the way before Sanchez shows up."

Jane Ann agreed and went to warm up the gravy. Frannie got a coffee refill and headed into her camper, followed by Donna.

"Can I help?"

"Sure," Frannie pulled a sack of potatoes from under one of the dinette benches. The two proceeded to scrub, pierce and microwave enough potatoes for the six of them plus several extra.

"I hope Sanchez is able to fill in a few gaps for us," Donna said.

"That would be nice," Frannie said. "And of course, it won't tie everything up in a nice little package. Stephanie may still have problems with Trey, Dave Schlumm may still be a jerk to his daughter, and Stub's vacation is still a nightmare." She got out a baking pan and placed the cooked potatoes on it.

"True. Now you smash them?" She watched as Frannie used a spatula to flatten each potato. Then Frannie directed Donna to drizzle each potato with olive oil and sprinkle them with salt and pepper while she called Larry into light the oven.

"Aren't those things a pain to light? We've hardly ever used ours," Donna said, watching Larry on his knees peering into the tiny oven with a lighter.

"Us either," Frannie said. "Only for smashed potatoes." She shoved the small pan in the oven, checked her watch, and said, "Twenty or twenty-five minutes."

They gathered plates and silverware and went back outside and proceeded to clean off the table. Rob went back to their trailer for juice and glasses. Mickey came up to Frannie while she set out plates.

"Hey, Fran, I'm awfully glad you're okay. I wasn't making light of what you went through. Jane Ann was beside herself with worry yesterday — well, me too."

"Mickey, don't you think I know after all these years that the more stressed you are, the more obnoxious you get?" She gave him a hug and he gave her a sheepish grin.

"Really? Is that what it is?"

"Of course."

"I'd better go help my wife."

"Excellent idea."

BEFORE LONG, MICKEY came out bearing a pan of sausage gravy, the potatoes were passed around, and they all settled to a more relaxed and pleasant meal than any since their arrival. The beautiful weather continued, and the morning sounds of the birds provided the perfect backdrop. When they finished and pronounced themselves unable to eat another bite that day — well, at least until supper since it was a late breakfast — Mickey and Rob offered to do the dishes. Frannie found an old foil tray and sent the remaining potatoes and gravy with Larry over to Stub and his friends.

They were just wiping off the table again and topping off their coffee cups when Agent Sanchez pulled up.

"Good morning, folks! Better than it's been anyway." They unanimously   agreed and offered him a chair, which he accepted, along with a cup of coffee. He pulled out a small recorder. "I hope you don't mind, but I need your statements recorded and I thought you would rather do this out here than at the police station."

"Yes, we would," Frannie said and Donna nodded too.

They all settled in the chairs. Agent Sanchez snapped on the recorder, gave his name, the date, and other pertinent details. Frannie and Donna proceeded to retell their tale, interrupted occasionally by perceptive questions from Sanchez. He was impressed by the women's escape attempts and their relative calm through the whole ordeal, although Frannie didn't remember being calm at all.

When they finished, he turned off his recorder and went to refill his cup. Mickey and Rob exited the Ferarro RV complaining about dishpan hands and rejoined the group.

"So, Ms. Shoemaker, how did you figure out the black market thing?"

"Marner had a weird reaction Saturday when the funeral director mentioned that Maeve Schlumm would be cremated—like he had reason to be pleased about it. Donna joked afterwards that maybe he was a body snatcher. That didn't really register at the time, but combined with his attempt to pick up Randy's things and the tissue services address in Randy's duffel, it was the only thing that made sense. I had seen a news report about the black market in tissue not long ago."

"So what's happened with Marner? Is he talking?" Larry asked.

"Non-stop," Sanchez said. "He's new at this, thought it would be a snap out here in the sticks, and that he was invulnerable. So now he's scared."

"So why did he kill Randy? That's the one thing we don't get," said Frannie.

"Apparently Randy got cold feet. When their trip was cut short, he put the cooler out for Marner to pick up again and used his GPS to mark it and gave Marner the coordinates. But the more he thought about it, the more scared he got. Poor guy was pretty stressed anyway. He had tax problems and saw this as a way out. Thought it was pretty harmless. Then Marner kills Maeve when he's making the drop. And when Randy goes to pick up the cooler, it's dark so he doesn't even see the body. Imagine his shock the next morning when you guys discover that."

"Stub has insisted all along that Randy wasn't a murderer," Larry said.

"And he wasn't," Sanchez continued. "So he was going to turn himself in and decided to use the cover of the storm to retrieve the cooler. However, he made the mistake of telling Marner that he was quitting. So Marner was waiting for him."

"I think Marner overheard Stub mention to me that Randy had a duffel bag and shaving kit. He must have come back here yesterday hoping he could sneak around the back of Stub's RV and somehow retrieve anything incriminating." Frannie said.

"The address list," Donna said.

"Yes, that was exactly it," Sanchez replied. "And that reminds me, the handwriting on that list appears to be the same person who wrote your note. We're having the state lab confirm that. But it appears that Randy tried to warn you off rather than threaten you—part of his attempt to make amends." Frannie tried to catch her husband's eye—a perfect 'I told you so' opportunity. Sanchez stood and returned his small recorder to his pocket. "Well, ladies, I hope you don't make a habit of this detective work or you could put me out of business."

"Believe me, Mr. Sanchez, we have no desire to repeat this," Frannie said. "We honestly did not intentionally get involved. We've been camping ten years or more and have never experienced anything like this. I don't expect we will again."

"So this weekend won't end your camping days?" Sanchez looked around the group.

They all looked at each other with surprise. No one had even considered not camping.

"Heavens, no," Jane Ann replied for the group. "We have a trip planned in two weeks to go biking in Minnesota with five other couples and we'll all be camping. The menu is to die for, in case you want to drop by," she finished with a grin.

"Out of my jurisdiction, I'm afraid."

223

Mickey added, "And we have state park reservations for four or five more weekends this summer and fall, plus we'll do several county parks."

The agent stood and placed his mug on the table. "Well, good luck to you all. And thanks again for your help." He looked directly at Frannie, Larry and Donna. "Stay safe." He walked back to his car.

They all waved goodbye and voiced thanks and farewells. He walked over to Stub's motorhome to give him a final report on Randy's death.

The campers stoked their fire and began to discuss plans to pack up and depart early afternoon. While they were talking, the sheriff's car pulled up and the sheriff along with Deputy Smith, Stephanie and River got out. River ran over to Mickey yelling, "What's on the radar?"

Mickey pulled out his phone, orchestrated a few flicks and swipes and turned the screen so River could see it.

"See? No green, no yellow, no red—going to be a beautiful day."

Stephanie came over to Frannie and Donna, who had stood to greet her. "I heard what happened. I'm so glad you guys are okay and that Trey wasn't a part of it."

"No, he wasn't," Frannie said, thinking that she hoped, for Stephanie and River's sake, he wasn't a part of something else.

"Did either of you get injured?"

"We're pretty stiff and sore and Frannie got a thorn in her palm," Donna said, and Frannie held up her sore hand. "Larry got the worst of it."

Stephanie looked over at Larry, who put on a sad sack face. Frannie said to her, "He's going to use this the rest of the summer to get waited on hand and foot."

To her surprise, Stephanie leaned over and hugged her gently. "You guys are great. I don't know what I would have done without you this weekend. Will you ever come back here again to camp?"

"Probably not this summer," Frannie said. "We have a lot of other places reserved. But this park is one of our favorites and we will be back."

Sheriff Ingrham and Deputy Smith walked over and inquired about their welfare today.

The sheriff said, "I'm glad to hear you say you're not going to write off our park based on this past weekend."

"If we only run into murder once every ten years," Larry said, "we should be okay for as long as we can handle this rig."

"I'd better go pack up my rig," Stephanie said. "River, are you going to help me?"

"Awww, I wanted to talk to Mickey."

"He's the only one," Jane Ann said. Mickey hoisted himself out of his chair.

"Rob, let's go help River get his stuff packed up. Then maybe we'll have time for a quick game of Chicken Feet."

"Oh boy!" River shouted. "Let's go." He raced around the Shoemakers' camper to his own site.

"We don't have to run like that, do we?" Rob asked Mickey.

"Not an issue because neither of us can," Mickey said. And off they went, much slower.

The sheriff tipped his hat and said, "Hope to see you in the future then, under pleasanter circumstances." He and the deputy got back in the patrol car. Agent Sanchez had moved his car on down to talk to Dave Schlumm, and with the road open again, Frannie could see signs of packing up all around them. The Airstream owners had returned, hooked up their trailer and were pulling out. Stub waved as he and his friends reloaded the storage compartments again. When they finished, he came over to say goodbye.

"Hey, I'm sorry that we really messed up your weekend," he began.

"Stub, as I told you before, this was in no way your fault. And you were right that Randy was not a murderer," Frannie said.

"That's nice of you. I've been thinking. I know I told you that no way I would ever do this again, but you guys have so much fun—when you aren't abducted, that is—I might try it again with just my family."

"Wonderful. But start small and stay close to home—see if you like it. You guys have given us a lot of entertainment this weekend." She smiled and Donna agreed.

Stub laughed. "Yeah, I'm sure we have. Well, good luck to all of you—and happy camping."

He shook hands with Larry and Frannie, but Donna leaned over and gave him a hug. His face turned bright red. "Gee…thanks." He turned and retreated to his side of the road.

Frannie looked at Donna and Jane Ann and they all struggled to contain their laughter. "Poor guy," said Jane Ann.

They started their packing up process. Frannie worked inside, stowing everything that might slide or move around. Toothbrushes, drinking glasses, and soap went back in the bathroom cabinet. The refrigerator was checked for anything that could spill. The clock, tissue box, and a little vase confined to cabinets or the footstool. Bedside lamps unplugged and laid on the bed, water pump and heater turned off, TV antenna cranked down. Finally, she and Larry slid his recliner near the door and they brought the slide in.

Outside, they stowed lawn chairs and empty firewood bins in the back of the pickup. Larry was collapsing their utility table and Frannie was returning some items to Jane Ann when Dave Schlumm appeared in their campsite.

"Good morning," he said as if he wasn't certain it was. Frannie didn't really want to talk to him since he had thrown his daughter out but they all stopped what they were doing and nodded to him.

"Wanted to talk especially to you," he inclined his head toward Frannie. She thought, 'Now, what?'

"Yes, Mr. Schlumm?" Perhaps a little coolly.

"Heard what you did yesterday and just want to thank you."

"What we did?"

"Stopping that monster from violatin' Maeve's body. Poor woman didn't deserve that after puttin' up with me."

"I can't take any credit for that, Dave—we were mostly trying to keep him from killing us."

"But you stopped him from hurting anybody else. That's good. I realize now that I drove off my daughter too. Going to try and patch that up. Just wanted you to know."

"I'm glad to hear that and we wish you the best."

"That's all I got to say. Looks like you're gettin' ready to pull out. Drive safe."

He turned and shuffled back towards his camper.

"Strange guy," said Larry, as they returned to their tasks. Before they were done, the bikers went by pulling their little trailers and waving gaily. By the time they got everything hooked up, the campground had pretty much emptied; after being confined for two days, people didn't want to take a chance on something else happening before they could head home. Mickey and Jane Ann led in their RV, then the Nowaks, with the Shoemakers in the rear. A final stop at the dump station and they wended their way slowly out of the park, shaded by the beautiful trees and limestone bluffs.

Perched up in the passenger seat of their truck with Cuba's head over her shoulder, Frannie said, "This is one camping weekend I'm not sad to put behind us."

Larry reached over and rubbed the back of her neck. "Babe, the odds are in our favor. Smoooth camping ahead."

Happy Camper Tips

Some of the recipes mentioned in Bats and Bones plus some useful tips while you're camping!

Happy Camper Tip #1

Poor Stub is not the first camper to get in the wrong spot. Often the numbers for two campsites will be on one post and you can't tell which is which unless you know what direction the numbering goes. It's worth a few minutes to check this out—easier than cranking the stabilizers up, bringing the slide in, removing the brakes, backing the truck up, hooking the trailer back up…you get the picture.

Happy Camper Tip #2

With gas prices on the rise, no one wants to have pull added water weight in their RV. Filling the tanks is best done after arrival at the campground. However, it's also best to make sure all of the faucets inside are turned off. Once, we filled our fresh water tank, drove around the campground deciding on a site, pulled in, set up, and went inside, only to find that the bathtub tap had been left open and most of the fresh water had drained into the grey water tank. We haven't done that again.

Happy Camper Tip #3

This suggestion came in one of those forwarded e-mails of household hints but is especially true when camping. Always have WD40 and duct tape. If something is supposed to move and doesn't, use WD40. If it's not supposed to move and does, use duct tape.

Happy Camper Tip #4

Marinated Cold Roast Beef: This easy recipe is excellent for picnics and parties also. Cook a beef roast in the oven to 140. Cool and slice as thin as possible. Pour over a marinade made of ½ cup oil, 1/3 cup lemon juice, minced garlic and lots of fresh rosemary. Chill and serve on bread or buns.

Happy Camper Tip #5

RVs, trailers and fifth wheels generally don't have a lot of wall space, but you may want to hang a picture or two without adding a heavy frame. You can use a pre-cut mat for this purpose and leave it plain or paint it or cover it with appropriate paper, such as birch bark wallpaper samples...gotten slowly over time from your favorite home improvement store. If you tent camp, you might want to consider a digital picture frame or forgo the décor.

Happy Camper Tip #6

Raccoons can open anything humans can devise. They once got in our cooler and stole a whipped topping container that actually had fishing worms in it. I imagine they were pretty disappointed when they opened it. Another time, they took all the juice boxes out of a cooler, emptied them and left them scattered on the ground. On still another occasion, they polished off a dozen ears of sweet corn soaking in a bucket, leaving only the husks. They also don't pick up after themselves. Eventually you learn to put everything edible in a vehicle or camper.

Happy Camper Tip #7

Bunge cords are the answer to everything that WD40 and duct tape won't fix. They will hold bikes on campers, lights on awnings, or pants up if you need a belt.

Happy Camper Tip #8

Many campers share Frannie and Larry's memory of a bad night with their awning. Awnings provide excellent shade and shelter from a gentle rain; most are large enough to drag a picnic table under. They also give campers a place to hang their really cute outdoor lights. But in high winds, they can act as a sail or be ripped from the camper, causing expensive repairs. An ounce of prevention, etc.

Happy Camper Tip #9

The biggest cause of clutter, especially when the grandchildren come along camping, is shoes. In the case of grandchildren, those shoes get bigger every year. Since campers are designed like boats to utilize every inch of space, there is nowhere to put shoes that they will not be in the way. We removed the door from a cabinet near the entrance and now all shoes go in there. No more senseless size 12 Nike accidents.

Happy Camper Tip #10

Glow Sticks: This wonderful invention is perfect for camping. Glow sticks can be formed into bracelets, necklaces, and dog collars to keep track of kids and pets in dark campgrounds. Kids can play tag with them and tape them to the spokes of their bikes. The only drawback is that my grandchildren believe they will last longer in the freezer, so it is not unusual for our freezer to rain glow sticks upon opening.

Happy Camper Tip #11

Herbed Garden Potato Salad: In a blender, combine ¾ cup oil, ½ cup cider or tarragon vinegar, 1 teaspoon of salt, 1 teaspoon onion powder, ½ teaspoon garlic powder and ¼ teaspoon pepper with fresh parsley and basil leaves. Blend until smooth.

Combine 6 cups cooked sliced potatoes, 3 cups cooked green beans, and 2 cups cooked sliced carrots.

Pour dressing over warm vegetables and chill. Great to make ahead because it keeps and travels well.

Happy Camper Tip #12

Chicken Feet is one of those table games with as many variations as there are contentious camping groups. We play with double-twelve dominoes, but any size set can be used. In our version, every player draws seven dominoes, placing the rest face down at the side of the table. The player with the highest double begins by placing that tile face up in the middle of the table, say a double twelve. Each player must then match another twelve to the first, three tiles on a side. If a player doesn't have a twelve, he or she must draw from the "bone yard." Sometimes, by the time the first six tiles are laid down, players may have gone from their original seven to fifteen or twenty. Once the first six are down, play can proceed by matching any tile in the player's 'hand' to an exposed end on the table. If a player cannot make a match, it's back to the bone yard.

To make a chicken foot, a player can lay down a double crosswise. The next three plays must match the double and are placed at angles to one side of the double to give the appearance of the bird's foot. No other tiles can be placed until the three forming the foot are laid down. No match? Draw again. The goal is to be the first one to get rid of one's tiles.

NOTE: It is important to yell "Chicken Feet!" when you put down a double, unless it's quiet hours in the campground. If it's after quiet hours, don't play this game.

Domino games work best on a plain picnic tablecloth; they tend to get lost on patterned ones.

Happy Camper Tip #13

Pie irons resemble a small square (usually) waffle iron without grids but with very long handles. They can be used to grill sandwiches or make 'pies' consisting of two pieces of bread with a fruit filling over an open fire. Very popular with children.

Happy Camper Tip #15

One of Iowa's most beautiful and best known state parks, Maquoketa Caves, is the basis for the fictitious Bat Cave State Park. There are amazing caves and trails and the campground is delightful. There is no old cabin or tunnel that I know of, and the campground hosts aren't crabby.

Happy Camper Tip #16

Smashed Potatoes and Sausage Gravy: Bake russet or red potatoes either in a conventional or microwave oven. Place on a greased cookie sheet and smash down with a spatula. (Good therapy when the raccoons have emptied your coolers or you found a body.) Drizzle with olive oil, salt and pepper, and bake about 20-30 minutes in a 400-degree oven until crisp. Serve with sausage gravy.

OTHER BOOKS BY THE AUTHOR

The award-winning Frannie Shoemaker Campground Mysteries:

The Blue Coyote: (An IndieBRAG Medallion honoree and a 2013 Chanticleer CLUE finalist) Frannie and Larry Shoemaker love taking their grandchildren, Sabet and Joe, camping with them. But at Bluffs State Park, another young girl disappears from the campground in broad daylight, and Frannie's fears increase. Accusations against Larry and her add to the cloud over their heads.

Peete and Repeat: (An IndieBRAG Medallion honoree, 2013 Chanticleer CLUE finalist, and 2014 Chanticleer Mystery and Mayhem finalist) A biking and camping trip to southeastern Minnesota turns into double trouble. Strange happenings in the campground, the nearby nature learning center, and an old power plant complicate the suspect pool and Frannie tries to stay out of it—really—but what can she do?

The Lady of the Lake: (An IndieBRAG Medallion honoree, 2014 Chanticleer CLUE finalist) A trip down memory lane is fine if you don't stumble on a body. Frannie Shoemaker and her friends camp at Old Dam Trail State Park and take in the county fair. But, Donna becomes the focus of a murder investigation and Frannie wonders if the police shouldn't be looking closer at the victim's many enemies.

To Cache a Killer: Geocaching isn't supposed to be about finding dead bodies. But when retiree, Frannie Shoemaker go camping, standard definitions don't apply. A weekend in a beautiful state park in Iowa buzzes with fund-raising events, a search for Ninja turtles, a bevy of suspects, and lots of great food — and a body.

A Campy Christmas: A Holiday novella. The Shoemakers and Ferraros plan to spend Christmas in Texas and then take a camping trip through the Southwest. But those plans are stopped cold when they are snowbound in a campground in Missouri.

The Space Invader: A cozy/thriller mystery! The starry skies over New Mexico, the "Land of Enchantment," may hold secrets of their own. The Shoemakers and the Ferraros, on an extended camping trip, find themselves picking up a souvenir they don't want and taking sidetrips they didn't plan on.

We are NOT Buying a Camper! A prequel to the Frannie Shoemaker Campground Mysteries. Frannie and Larry Shoemaker have busy jobs, two teenagers, and plenty of other demands on their time and sanity. Larry's sister and brother-in-law pester them to try camping for relaxation--time to sit back, enjoy nature, and catch up on naps. After all, what could go wrong? Join Frannie as "RV there yet?" becomes

"RV crazy?" and she learns that going back to nature doesn't necessarily mean a simpler life.

Happy Camper Tips and Recipes: All of the tips and recipes from the first four Frannie Shoemaker books in one convenient paperback or Kindle version that you can keep in your camping supplies!

The Time Travel Trailer Series

The Time Travel Trailer: (A Chanticleer 2015 Cygnus award finalist) A 1937 vintage camper trailer half hidden in weeds catches Lynne McBriar's eye when she is visiting an elderly friend Ben. But after each remodel, sleeping in the trailer lands Lynne and her daughter Dinah in a previous decade — exciting, yet frightening.

Trailer on the Fly: (An IndieBRAG Medallion Honoree) How many of us have wished at some time or other we could go back in time and change an action or a decision or just take back something that was said? But it is what it is. There is no rewind, reboot, delete key or any other trick to change the past, right?

Lynne McBriar can. She buys a 1937 camper that turned out to be a time portal. When she meets a young woman who suffers from serious depression over the loss of a close friend ten years earlier, she has the power to do something about it. And there is no reason not to use that power. Right?

THANKS...

For taking your time to share Frannie and Larry's adventures. Just as the sound of a tree falling in the forest depends on hearers, a book doesn't matter if it has no readers. Please consider sharing your thoughts with other readers in a review on Amazon.com.

My website at www.karenmussernortman.com provides updates on my books, my blog, and photos of our for-real camping trips. You can also sign up for my email list for a monthly update on upcoming free books and other information.

ACKNOWLEDGMENTS

No creative effort takes place in total isolation and this book is no exception. I wish to thank John and Shannon, for information on funeral homes and state park operation and Ginge and Marcia for being my early readers, and giving tremendous feedback. And to my siblings: Gretchen, who did the cover artwork; Libby, who designed the cover; and Jim, who did the final read-through and found a couple of serious clinkers, I'm sorry I ever wished to be an only child. To my other friends and family for encouragement, and my husband Butch for continuing support, my undying gratitude.

ABOUT THE AUTHOR

Karen Musser Nortman, after previous incarnations as a secondary social studies teacher (22 years) and a test developer (18 years), returned to her childhood dream of writing a novel. *Bats and Bones*, a cozy mystery, came out of numerous 'round the campfire' discussions, making up answers to questions raised by the peephole glimpses one gets into the lives of fellow campers. Where did those people disappear to for the last two days? What kinds of bones are in this fire pit? Why is that woman wearing heels to the shower house?

Karen and her husband Butch originally tent camped when their children were young and switched to a travel trailer when sleeping on the ground lost its romantic adventure. They take frequent weekend jaunts with friends to parks in Iowa and surrounding states, plus occasional longer trips. Entertainment on these trips has ranged from geocaching and hiking/biking to barbecue contests, balloon fests, and buck skinners' rendezvous. Frannie and Larry will no doubt check out some of these options on their future adventures.

Karen has three children and eight grandchildren. She also loves reading, gardening, and knitting, and can recite the 99 counties of Iowa in alphabetical order.

Made in the USA
Columbia, SC
29 January 2021

31836138R00152